ANICE

The Cursed Clan

MELISSA SCHROEDER

Edited by
NOEL VARNER

Illustrated by
SCOTT CARPENTER

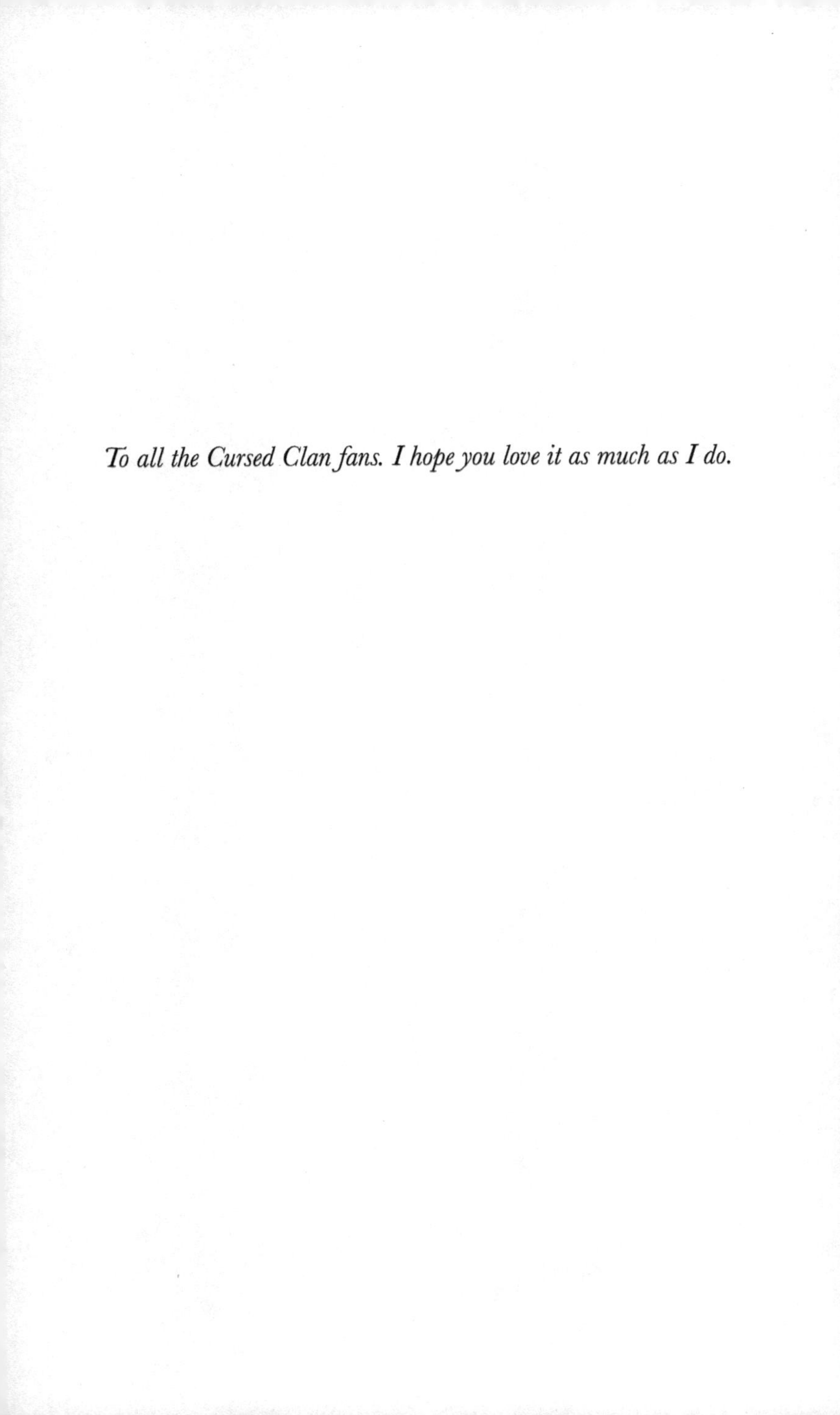

To all the Cursed Clan fans. I hope you love it as much as I do.

Acknowledgments

First, I want to thank all the usual suspects. Noel Varner for editing, working hard and pushing me to make the book even better. Thanks to the two best friends a girl could have, Joy Harris and Brandy Walker. Also, a shout out to Scott Carpenter for the beautiful covers. A big thanks to my husband Les for encouraging me to finish up the series.

Now, to all you Cursed Clan fans: Thank you. I know this is not one of my blockbuster series, but it is one of my favs. And I know those of you who truly love it, LOOOOOOOVE IT. I forgive all the threats to do me bodily harm and will only remember that all of you love the McLennans as much as I do.

Contents

Prologue

Anice lay in the field, looking up at the starry night. It was late, later than a lass like her should be out, but she didn't care. Her brother and her cousins could galivant all over the countryside at all hours of the day or night, but her following suit was frowned upon. She was sick of playing by the rules.

So, there she lay, the soft grass beneath her body and the entire sky above her. She couldn't fight the pull of the night. It always seemed to grab hold of her, especially when the moon was full. She could stare up at it for hours, waiting. For what, she had no idea, but anticipation always seemed to grow during this time of the month.

A twig snapped, and Anice stilled. She did as her cousin Callum had taught her and listened. More rustling. Not the wind and definitely bigger than most of the nocturnal animals in the area. Her instinct told her to run as fast as she could, but a voice stopped her.

"Lady Anice, do not fret," an older, weary voice called out to her. When the person came into view, Anice recognized her. The witch who told fortunes and saved lives.

"I wasn't fretting," she lied. "What are you doing out and about this late?"

"I could ask the same of you, but I know why you are here." She sighed. "Frederica had a baby tonight and I attended the birthing."

She nodded but said nothing else. Anice wanted to ask the woman more, to know everything about her future, but she controlled the urge…barely.

"I should get home before I am missed," she said, brushing the grass and twigs from her plaid. "Good eve."

She took three steps before the witch called out to her, "Don't you want to know your future, Lady Anice?"

Anice hated the fact that she did. More than anything in the world right now. She turned to face the witch. "I doona think that is a good idea."

"Why is that?"

"Knowing what has been foretold might hinder my true nature."

There was a long pause, then the witch threw back her head and cackled.

"Stop that," Anice said, trying to ignore how embarrassed she was. "I said, *stop it.*"

The witch finally calmed herself. "Please, do not take offense, my lady. I was only enjoying your spirit. Too many women don't have your courage. Tis good, since you will be needing it."

Unable to resist, she stepped closer. "So, you *do* know my future?"

"No. Not completely. The Fates do not always reveal their ways to me."

"But you know something?"

The older woman's smile faded, and her expression grew troubled. "Yes. For all of us in the Highlands. We will be forced to endure some of the worst times we have seen in centuries. But for you, your mate…he will not be easy."

She snorted. "I would not want an easy man. They are usually lazy."

The witch nodded, once. "You are as wise as I thought. Tis good because this man in your future is just like you."

"Like me, how?"

"Tell me, my lady. Why do you like to come outside at night?"

"Tis quiet. I like that everything seems so serene at night."

The witch nodded. "But I guess you specifically come out during the cycle that features a full moon."

"Maybe." But it was true. It was always this night that called to her.

"Yes. Well, your mate will need you by his side, *and* he will need a woman who understands."

"Understands that he traipses across the fields at night?" She crossed her arms beneath her breasts. "What are you blathering on about?"

Another quick smile, then it faded. "Oh, how I would want to see you fall in love, but I fear it will be long after I am gone from this earth."

Intrigued even more, she stepped closer. "How long?"

"I cannae tell you that."

"Then what good are you?" she asked, frustration threading her tone. Anice knew it was unladylike to be so blunt, but she didn't care.

For a long moment, the witch said nothing. The silence filled the night and Anice suddenly felt as if Nanny had caught her stealing biscuits.

She opened her mouth to apologize, but the witch held up her hand.

"No, you need that attitude, my lady. You are the key and it will test you."

"The key?"

"The link between families. You are the one who will save the Clans, the *only* one who can unite them."

She rolled her eyes.

"Doona think lightly of your role. Your mate and you will have a difficult time of it. He will be true to you, Anice. A man that might not seem to be, but he is. Believe in him, and you can have a happy life."

"But if I don't?"

The sadness in the witch's eyes stole Anice's breath. Fear threaded through her veins as she tried to take in air. It was as if she were being slowly drowned.

"Oh, my lady...I would rather not say."

Anger replaced her panic. "Tell me."

The witch sighed. Regret danced on the air around them. "Destruction of everything you hold dear."

Chapter One

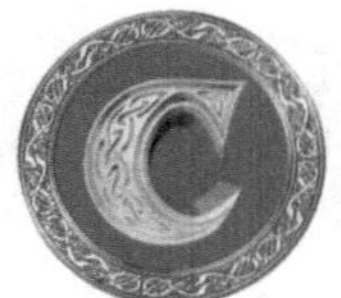

Anice stood in her walk-in closet and tried to figure out what to wear for the evening. She felt like such a loser because she couldn't find anything. True, this was the fifth date with Brody, but she shouldn't be this indecisive. Was it because she had decided tonight was the night to seduce him?

She rolled her eyes. "Like I know how to do that."

"Speaking to yourself again, sister?" Rena asked, appearing beside her.

"Bloody hell, I told you not to do that."

Her soon to be sister-in-law smiled. "I'm sorry but your thoughts were kind of shouty."

Half fae/half human, Rena had the ability to hear others' thoughts; although, she had learned to block out the thoughts of others.

She sighed. "I'm sorry for being shouty." she couldn't fight the smile that danced around her lips. "I'm nervous about tonight."

"Another date with the Brody man?"

She nodded. Her brother and cousins weren't overly

happy about it, but after a couple of centuries, she figured she deserved a little fun.

"We're going to dinner tonight, and he insisted on picking me up this time."

"What time?"

"Seven."

Rena frowned. "I have to go to some kind of fundraiser benefit with your brother or I would check him out."

"I don't think you need to. Normal human." Normal, sexy human. One that made her want to eat him up with one big bite.

"Ooch, stop," Rena said holding her head.

"Sorry. I just can't stop thinking about him."

"Hmm."

"What's that supposed to mean?"

"That means there was a man that I couldn't stop thinking about at one time."

"And?"

Her expression softened. "I'm marrying him next month."

Panic tickled the back of her throat. She didn't need this complication. She just needed to have an affair. Feelings were okay, unless she got wrapped up in him. She didn't want that problem.

"Are you trying to tell me I'm in love with Brody?"

"Falling in love."

Anice sighed.

"You have a problem with this, sister?" Rena asked.

"I just don't want that issue. I just want to...well, you know."

"You want a good hard shag," Rena said, humor filling

her tone. "I definitely agree with that. Still, I want to meet him soon."

"Why?"

"You're my sister, Anice. I want to know the man who is stealing your heart."

"Thanks for that. My brother and cousins seem to think I can't be trusted."

Of course, there was a very good reason for that. She had been duped by one of the McWaltons decades earlier. She knew they had all been upset at the time, and she had been left devastated. It had taken her months to return to normal and since then she hadn't had a relationship. She feared they continued to see her as that same broken woman.

"You're not."

"What?"

"Broken. I truly apologize, but I can't fight your thoughts. You might not be my blood, but you are to be my sister by marriage and that connects us. I love you as much as I love Maggie and Meghan."

She felt the backs of her eyes burn. For Rena to admit such a thing, Anice knew that made her special. Rena didn't let a lot of people into her life.

"Don't cry."

"I can't help it," Anice said with a laugh. "It's your fault."

Rena studied her for a second, then she opened her arms. Anice accepted the hug, something uncommon for Rena. Affection wasn't easily given—except with Maggie and Meghan. Now, that had extended to Anice and she relished it. It was so insanely cool to have a sister.

"Sister, you are strong, probably the strongest of all your kin. You might not see it or feel it, but you are."

"And my brother and cousins?"

"They are idiot men who can't be trusted for their opinions."

She pulled back, laughing. "You're marrying one of them."

"True, but this is part of their makeup. It's instinctual. I know that Phoebe could give you a better explanation, but they feel the need to protect. It's important to them that they make sure you are safe."

"I know, and I love them for that, but it is so annoying."

"I completely understand. When Fletcher stepped in front of me to protect me from a bullet, I wanted to strangle him."

"I think you should go sexy tonight."

"You think?"

She nodded. "I think you need to move this thing along or you'll explode from never having sex."

Anice chuckled. "There is that."

"What are you planning in the way of lingerie?"

Anice wasn't a prude, but she wasn't accustomed to having someone being so nosey about her underwear.

"Um, a bra and panties."

Rena rolled her eyes. "Show me."

"I have it on." She was wearing a robe over her bra and panties.

Rena made a motion with her hands. "Come on. It's not like I haven't seen what you have. I have the same bits and pieces."

Anice sighed. "It's just a bra and panties, and I don't know why we're discussing this."

"Because, you are planning on letting him see beneath your clothes tonight. You want to make sure you have something on to entice him. You should wear this," she said grabbing a purple dress. It was one of her favorites, as the color of the dress made her skin look amazing and brought out the deep blue in her eyes.

"Yeah?"

Rena nodded. "Looks fabulous on you. Plus, it isn't overly revealing but just enough. Driving him crazy about what is beneath will get him even more interested in finding out."

"Okay."

"Hair up."

She wiggled her fingers and all of a sudden, Anice's hair was up in a very intricate style, with a few curls left down.

"Whoa. I should become a witch."

Rena smiled. "The M and M's are very good at it. I'm better."

"We hear you," Maggie said as she walked in with Meghan by her side.

"Where's Phoebe?" she asked sarcastically.

"Napping."

Their cousin's wife was in the last six weeks of her pregnancy. She had been taking a lot of naps in between deciphering the diary.

"Wow, I guess Rena did your hair?" Meghan said.

She nodded.

"And I agree with the purple dress. You also need to wear stockings tonight."

Anice frowned. "I'm not a fan."

"No, but men are. Just the idea that you are wearing stockings might drive him even crazier."

"What color are your bra and panties? Do you have matching garters?" Meghan said, leaving them in the walk-in closet. The other two trailed after her and Anice blinked. Was she going to go through her drawers looking for garters?

"Oh, look at these."

Bloody hell. She hurried after them and found all three of them looking at a pair of garters.

"Hey," she said. The three women turned in unison, as if it were a choreographed event. If she wasn't so embarrassed, she would have laughed.

"What's wrong?" Maggie asked.

"Do you do this to everyone you know? Just go through their stuff and make comments."

Maggie blinked, then she gave her an understanding smile. "I'm sorry. I forget that you virtually spent all this time without any women around. You've never dealt with the sisterhood kind of moments."

"So this is normal?"

"Well, no one would call Maggie here normal," Meghan said with a laugh.

"Go get bent, Meg."

"It is normal for women, though, to share things like this."

"Well, I guess...I've seen it in movies, but..."

Rena came forward and slipped an arm around her. "I understand, sister. You've had none of these moments. You've been the only girl and couldn't share your secrets with anyone other than your obtuse cousins."

"It hasn't been that bad," she said.

"You handled it better than I would have," Maggie said, crossing her arms beneath her breasts. She was a tiny woman in stature, just reaching Anice's shoulders, but she was big in personality. All of her sisters were, at this point.

She held that term to her heart. She had only one

sibling, her twin Fletcher. She had never had a close female friend, let alone four--if she counted Phoebe, and she did. It still didn't make it any easier to deal with the way they infiltrated her life. To them, it was normal. To her, she felt as if she had been invaded.

"Either way, what color do you have on?"

"She said white," Rena said.

"I think you should go with black."

"Why?"

"Maybe all of you might think I'm crazy," Meghan said.

"We already do," Maggie said with a wicked smile.

"Suck it," Meghan said. Then she turned back to Anice. "There is an air of innocence about you. The black will be the exact opposite, you know what I mean. It's seductive, plus, you have the most amazing skin for someone who is over 200 years old--which I say is not fair at all--and it will look fantastic against the darker fabric."

"Oh, yeah, she's right," Maggie said.

Before she could respond, there was a knock at her door, then it swung open. Phoebe waddled in, a frown marring her usually sunny disposition. She made her way across Anice's bedroom and then stopped in front of the group. She put fisted hands on her hips. She was dressed in a robe and slippers, as she was a lot of the time these days.

"What the bloody hell is going on and why wasn't I called?"

"We're trying to get Anice laid," Maggie said.

There was a moment of stunned silence, then Phoebe giggled.

"That is a good idea, in my not so humble opinion," Phoebe said.

"You're not humble?" Anice asked.

"With the amount of degrees that I have, it is impossible. So," she said sitting down on the bed, "what have you ladies come up with?"

"Purple dress, stockings, and black lingerie."

"Oh, yeah. That would be wonderful. What are you two doing tonight?"

"Just a night out for dinner."

"And he's coming here to pick you up?" Anice nodded. "Brave too."

"Brave?"

"Would you want to deal with four very grumpy men who see it as their duty to protect you?"

"No. Only three. We have that benefit in town," Rena said. The McLennan's didn't go out often, but when they did, it was usually Anice's brother Fletcher. Now that he had Rena by his side, Anice no longer had to deal with those things.

"Still. I know that Callum has been grumpy about it all day."

"He can just get over it," Anice said.

"That's what I told him," Phoebe said.

"Either way, I will take your suggestions to heart," she said.

"Did Rena do your hair?" Phoebe asked.

"Yes."

"Figures. At the moment, I can't do a thing with my hair. I don't have the energy or the patience."

There was a flash and Phoebe's hair was in the neat chignon she usually wore. Once a tangled mess, it was now smooth and sleek.

"Thank you," she said.

"No problem. Just tell me if you need help with that

again," Rena said. "I think we should leave Anice to get ready for her date."

"Okay," Maggie said, walking forward and giving Anice a kiss on the cheek. Both Meghan and Rena followed suit. She was finally left alone with Phoebe. Her cousin-in-law sat on the bed, her feet dangling off the edge. They were swollen, as were her ankles.

"Does Callum know you're in here?"

Phoebe's husband, and the laird of the Clan, had been acting overprotective of his wife and their new baby. It was understandable. She was carrying the first known baby to be born to them since the curse had been enacted. There had also been a passage warning them about the next generation. Everyone's level of worry had heightened in the last few weeks, as they moved closer to the birth. Anice just hoped she could live up to the task of getting the last jewel.

"I'm a grown woman. I can walk around on my own." She patted the bed beside her. Anice walked over and sat down.

"What's wrong?"

"I've deciphered a little bit more in the diary I think has to do with you."

"Why didn't you say anything in front of the others?"

"Because you already have so much stress on you being the last."

She sighed and nodded. Phoebe pulled out a scrap of paper and unfolded it.

"The best of the five, the one with the truest heart, is the one who will decide their fate. She is the connection to everything that could save them from themselves."

Anice blinked. "How do you know that's about me?"

"First, you are the only one left. It also mentions the

amethyst, and I have heard all of the cousins and your brother make that remark about you."

"What remark?"

"You are the best of them. They have all said it one way or another. Anice...you are the key to all of this."

"I don't understand."

"You need to contemplate your role in this entire story. You're the one who kept the idea of ending the curse alive. You are the one who is the gentlest of hearts, but also the bravest."

Embarrassed, she shook her head. "Don't go barmy on me, Phoebe. I need at least one of us to stay sane."

Phoebe shook her head. "You are the bravest. I still cannot understand how you handled traipsing around all your idiot cousins and idiot brother all these years. The fear, the absolute terror of being a woman in those times..." she shook her head. "It's still not fantastic, but throughout the last two centuries, we have come a long way."

Again, the backs of her eyes burned, and she tried to blink the tears away. They fell down her cheeks nonetheless.

"Oh, sweet Anice, don't cry. It's all going to work out."

Anice nodded, not truly convinced. For the first time in all the years they had been pursuing this idea, she was starting to doubt it would conclude the way she wanted or hoped. And worse, they had no idea what was going to happen to Phoebe or her unborn bairn if Anice failed.

Phoebe took Anice's hand in hers. "I know it's scary, but there is a different way the witches talk about you. They talk about you as if you are the most precious of gifts. It's almost as if they revere you as some kind of goddess."

Anice snorted and Phoebe chuckled.

"I know you might not believe it, but you are. They call you the key. I just need to figure out what that key means. Key to what?"

"I've never heard anything about a key."

"Nor I in any of my translations. The barmy witches seem to have some hold over the book."

"What do you mean?"

"It seems I gravitate to a passage or two when they want me to. There is no rhyme or reason for the way I'm working through the book. Instead, I flip through the pages and they tell me where to stop."

"Odd," Anice murmured.

"Right?" She sighed. "Anyway, I just want you to forget all of this and go have fun tonight. Kiss the man, and much more if the mood strikes. You deserve it."

"I will."

"Now, help me up."

Anice did just as there was a knock on the door before it slammed open. Phoebe's husband Callum stood in the doorway, his regular scowl in place.

"You know I could have been naked, Callum."

He tossed an irritated look in Anice's direction before zeroing in on his wife. "I couldn't find you."

"Apparently you could, because here you are."

His frown turned darker. "You should be in bed."

"The doctor said a little walking was good."

"Not alone."

Phoebe rolled her eyes. "Have fun tonight," she said before kissing Anice on the cheek.

Before she could take another step, Callum was by her side. He took her hand and led her out of the room. Anice smiled and shut the door behind them, then leaned against it. It was hard to believe how fast their lives had changed, thanks to hiring Phoebe. Most people would say being immortal would be fun, but they never had much fun. Living year after year, watching those people you care about die, or worse, the need to cut yourself off from people so you are not hurt.

She sighed and pushed those thoughts aside. Tonight was about fun and seduction and nothing else.

Chapter Two

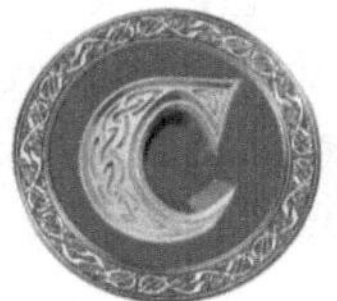

Brody Stewart looked at himself in the mirror and tried his best not to be nervous. It's not like he was a virgin. He'd lost that decades earlier or he would definitely be barmy by now. Their kind didn't do well going for long periods of celibacy. Maybe that's why he was such a mess at the moment.

One whole month. It seemed like a lifetime since he'd started dating Anice. As with every time before, thinking her name left him a bit weak. It wasn't odd for his kind to experience this, especially since he had yet to take her to his bed. But the intensity bothered him. She was his mate, but it wasn't as if she was the only woman who could be his mate. He'd met a few along the way, but with Anice, he seemed to get the shakes every time he thought of her. He felt like an alcoholic needing a pint to cure his need. Only, he didn't think a little taste would do the trick. There was a very good chance he would fall into bed with her and lose himself for days. Not a bad thing in point of fact.

His phone buzzed in his pocket and he hesitated. He really didn't want to deal with his cousin Gavin McWalton. Other than the fact that his cousin still thought Brody was doing this for him, Brody couldn't stand the bastard. He also didn't trust the other man's fixation on Anice. Why the hell had so many of his family seemed to be obsessed with her, he didn't know. It had lasted for centuries, and each generation worked against the McLennans. But there was always one laird, every now and then, who would become obsessed with Anice.

A growl rumbled in his chest as possessiveness flooded his blood.

She is ours.

As he attempted to ignore his wolf, Brody rolled his shoulders but couldn't fight the need vibrating within him. She tempted him in the worst way, and he needed to keep his head about him. He didn't need to lose his perspective, but he found himself drawn to her more and more. If she lived in town, he would probably spend every possible moment with her.

The fact that she was his mate further complicated things. He shut his eyes and tried his best to ignore the primal need to challenge his cousin. Gavin wanted to possess her in a way that was unnatural. It didn't make sense. Not really. He had been a normal man, just living his life. In fact, Gavin had been more accepting of Brody's arm of the family tree. Then, he had become the Laird. Since that moment, he had slowly tipped off the deep end into weird behavior. All of Gavin's machinations against the McLennans took a back seat to humiliating Anice.

"You think too much," Cayden said from behind him.

Brody looked at his brother's reflection in the mirror. Older by only thirteen months, they were closer than other brothers in other packs. As Alpha, Cayden was supposed to keep himself separate. At least, that was what occurred in other packs. It would never be that way with the Stewarts. It was impossible after what they had been through.

"I don't think too much. Thinking is just part of my job."

As Beta and helper to the Alpha, Brody's position was to make sure every plan had been thought out.

"I don't know why you think we need this."

He turned to face his brother. People said they looked so alike they could be twins. Well, except that Brody now sported a beard, and Cayden's facial scar set him apart. Usually, those marks would have faded. They tended to heal faster than their human counterparts, but there was one claw mark left. It sliced down his face. To this day, Brody was surprised Cayden didn't lose his eye.

"You sanctioned the action. Are you against it now?"

He shook his head. "But I do believe that we have other ways of gaining back our land. I don't trust Gavin."

He snorted. "None of us do. The man is definitely getting barmy."

"More than usual?"

He nodded. "You remember he was kind of odd as a child, but not anything to worry about. When he gained control of his Clan, he started plotting. Recently, he's become obsessed with Anice."

"Understandable. She's a gorgeous woman."

His chest rumbled.

Ours, his wolf proclaimed.

Cayden studied him for a long moment. "Whoa, brother, maybe you should take a few days away from the woman. You're getting too attached."

The idea of being away from Anice caused a shot of pain to lance through his body. She was his mate, he was sure of it now. They had not consummated the act, but he had definitely gotten attached. It wasn't like he couldn't find another mate. There wasn't just one mate for every wolf, but never before had he been this attached to a woman.

"No. We need to see this through. We need to bring the others home."

His brother nodded. Most of their family had scattered centuries ago. Wolves were no longer indigenous to Scotland, so if they did not have their own lands, they couldn't hide. Most of them had gone to Ireland or the Americas, but their homeland tugged at them constantly. Living apart like this was painful to all of them.

"There are other ways, Brody. I could approach Robertson Clan Pack."

"That would mean you would marry someone you did not love, and we would have to work with the Robertsons. I don't trust them any more than I trust Gavin."

They had been at odds with their old neighbors for a few decades. A truce would allow them some freedom, but he didn't like the fact that his brother would have to make the sacrifice. He had already sacrificed too much.

"While you betray a woman you are falling in love with?"

Brody hated the look his brother was giving him. He knew that he had taken liberties with Anice. That he should have walked away, but he couldn't, not without hurting himself, he had been a coward. For this one time in his life, he wanted to take the time.

"You know Gavin is going to think something is up. Maybe we could bring Esme in for a spell or two."

The cousin on the witchy side of their family still lived in the area. Another blessing was that she wanted to maim and/or kill every laird of the McWalton Clan. Her side of the family hadn't been treated any better than his.

"I don't know if we should make her a target."

Cayden nodded. "We have options, so remember that. Before you make any moves, the pack is important, but our souls are just as important. If you do anything to Anice, then you would definitely lose her. Having the land isn't important to me if you lose yourself in this fight." He studied Brody. "Why are you so nervous tonight?"

"I'm meeting the family."

"You work for the family. They know you."

"I'm picking her up at the mansion."

As a long moment of silence passed, Brody had to fight the urge to fidget. "You're declaring."

"No. I'm just making a point."

But he knew that was a lie. He knew that when he had insisted, he hadn't been in control. His wolf had come to life with a vengeance.

You just don't know what you need, his wolf whispered.

Shut up, you idiot.

"Listen, while this has been fun, I thought maybe I should show up on time."

A smile curled Cayden's lips and for a brief second, he reminded Brody of the brother he had known before the accident. "You seem particularly antsy tonight."

Because Anice had been increasingly overt in her need. More than once she had tried to entice him to take her home with him. If he did that, he'd have no way to control himself. It was just impossible for a wolf in heat.

Ease your needs. She's yours.

Bloody hell. His wolf was getting worse by the day.

"Gavin called me earlier. He's getting more and more insistent."

"What I don't understand is how seducing Anice would help him."

"I think he thinks my bedding Anice would give him some power over her."

"Again, still makes no sense. If he were doing the bedding, then I could understand."

He knew that was true, but it seemed easy enough when Gavin had first approached him about it. She was a beautiful woman and an enemy of his cousin's Clan. Once he got close to her though, he had known he had made a mistake. She was his mate, and while they said there wasn't one mate for every wolf, Brody couldn't imagine wanting another woman. *Ever*. And that scared the bloody hell out of him. Still, the need to be with her tugged at him constantly.

"Either way, I have a date tonight and I need to get going."

His brother nodded.

"Anything else?" he asked, anxious to get out of the room. He couldn't tell his brother that he was plotting another path. Brody knew that Anice was some kind of key to whatever Gavin was plotting. If Brody could figure it out, then he might be able to discover a way to get their land back and not betray Anice. He hadn't told his brother; although, he had a feeling that Cayden knew he was plotting something.

His brother shook his head. "Be safe."

Unsettled by the knowing look his brother gave him, Brody said nothing else as he left his room. Being late to the McLennans was not an option. He hurried down the steps and out the door of their house. It was a far cry from the mansion they had spent their early years in, but he liked it. In fact, he liked living in town now. He liked the hustle and bustle of the streets and easy access to things he liked. He enjoyed city life, even so, he knew they needed to be careful. It wasn't like his time in America where roaming just outside a major city would go unnoticed. People would notice a wolf running the perimeter of a city in Scotland.

He was about to pull out of the driveway when his phone buzzed again. Dammit. He knew he couldn't ignore Gavin because his cousin would just show up.

"What?"

Gavin was apparently taken aback by the growl in his voice.

"Is that the way you answer the phone all the time?"

"Only when you're about to make me late for a date with Anice."

"That's exactly what I wanted to talk to you about."

Brody said nothing because he could not bring himself to. He could not openly deceive Anice. First, he didn't want to. Second, he couldn't. As she was his mate, deceiving her would be painful, even deadly. They hadn't mated yet, or it would be worse.

"Yes? I thought we covered this earlier today."

"We did, but I wanted to make sure that you bedded the bitch soon."

Tell him to bugger off.

"I told you that it wasn't going to be that easy. Anice is very guarded, as many of our ancestors found out."

"*My* ancestors didn't truly understand her place in our history."

He ignored the growl from his wolf. He was from the same line, albeit some of it questionable. Truth was with witches on one side and wolves on the other, Brody knew they would never be in line for control of the Clan. But the fact was, he didn't want it, nor did his brother. They wanted their pack back on their lands and safe from hunters. For that, he would work through this mess.

Besides, each little nugget of information garnered him another hint of what Gavin was up to.

"I get that, but I need to make sure I make it there on time. I'm meeting her at the house tonight."

There was another long pause. "Indeed? Well, that's promising. I'll let you go, but make sure you report in to me."

Then he hung up without saying goodbye. Brody clicked off his phone and dropped it on the passenger seat. As he pulled out of the driveway, he made his way toward the Lennon mansion. He had never lived in such lavish surroundings. They had always been a small pack, not big enough to threaten others, but large enough that they could stand their ground. That is until one of Gavin's cousins from way back had thrown them off the land. They had been a pack without a homeland, and when Cayden tried to challenge the Robertsons, he had been left marked for life. Now he was talking about going back to them? Not acceptable.

He turned onto the road that lead to Anice's home. The closer he got the more he felt his wolf pacing, need rising. It wasn't just sexual, although there was that aspect. This pacing had more to do with the need to be near her. If he ever consummated, he would find it almost impossible to leave her side until she accepted their mating.

He rolled his shoulders again, trying to get his wolf to settle down.

Bed our mate and I will settle.

"Bloody hell. I'll never be able to bed her if I don't get there. Settle down so I can get through meeting the family."

His wolf gave him an unsatisfactory half growl/half sigh. He might not be happy about the situation, but he would apparently let Brody handle tonight.

As he parked in front of their mansion, he closed his eyes and tried to calm himself. It's dinner with a beautiful woman. She was his mate, yes, but more importantly, this was her family, and he had to impress them.

With that in mind, he opened his eyes and grabbed his phone as it started vibrating.

Esme: Don't compromise yourself tonight, Brody.

Damned witch.

Brody: I'm decades past my deflowering, cousin.

Esme: Stop that. I am serious. Anice is more important than you or I understand.

Brody: Talking in riddles irritates me. You know that.

Esme:…

His wolf paced and started to growl.

Between his family and his wolf, he would be the one they started to call barmy.

Then his phone rang, Esme's picture popping up on the screen.

"What?"

"Oh, look at you, being an ass."

"I'm at Anice's family mansion. I'm here to meet her family."

"Just…we have to figure this out, Brody. She's your mate and you cannot deceive her. It could ruin you."

"What do you mean?"

"Wolves who do that tend to go feral. Most of them have to be put down."

Bloody hell. Of course, part of him knew that. It was probably why he hadn't taken her to bed...even though he really, really wanted to.

"I've never heard that."

"Because it rarely happens. Just...tell her."

"That I'm a McWalton?"

"You are *not* a McWalton. You are a bloody Stewart."

He smiled. "Yes. But related to them."

"Yes. Just think about telling her. She is going to be angry but do it and then we can go from there."

He sighed. "I'll think about it. I have to go, Esme."

"Okay. Love you."

"Love you."

He clicked off his phone.

"Remember, behave."

Bed our mate, and I'll behave.

"I'm working on it," he muttered as he slipped out of the car.

Chapter Three

A nice was already waiting for Brody when he pulled into the driveway. She grabbed her coat and purse, hoping that she could hurry them both out of there before her cousins realized what was happening.

"You're not trying to keep us from talking to Brody, are you?" Angus asked from library as she passed by it.

Bollocks.

"No. And it's not like you can't talk to him at work."

But none of them had. They had kept out of it because they would not address personal things at work. If she'd had her choice, they would have never found out, but Brody had insisted on picking her up at the house tonight.

The doorbell rang and Belvidore was already walking toward the door. Dammit. There was no way out of it now. She followed the butler to the door and smiled when he opened it.

God, Brody was such a pretty man. From the moment she had met him, she had been intrigued. His work ethic was another part of his attraction. Still, if he had been lazy, Anice wasn't sure she would be deterred. She hated anyone who didn't do their job properly, but with Brody, she wasn't sure it would matter to her. He was dressed in a suit for the night, complete with tie. The steel gray suit made his eyes even more prominent. She wasn't a woman who usually liked beards, but Brody had grown one over the last month and she loved it. It made him look a little wild…and dangerous.

"Anice," he said as he stepped into the house. He looked at something over her shoulder and smiled. She assumed that it was for Angus, but when she glanced back, she inwardly groaned. Everyone had gathered in the massive hallway. Well, everyone but Phoebe. She was resting upstairs, exhausted from her translation work for the day.

She was going to kill them all. Well, except Jack. She turned back to Brody, then turned to face her family, waiting for him to step up beside her. When he did, she linked her arm with his.

She leaned closer and did her best not to sniff him. He always smelled of fresh sea air and heather. It was an odd combination, but it appealed to her just the same. "Sorry about this."

"Doona worry. I told you I've a very nosey family."

She nodded. She had yet to meet them, as he said most of them did not live in Scotland anymore, but it was one of the things they had bonded over.

"Everyone, this is Brody. Brody, you know the idiots who work at the company."

"Hey," Logan said with a laugh.

"But you might not know their very better halves.

Meghan is Logan's long-suffering wife," she said waving toward her cousin-in-law. "And this is Maggie and her son Jack."

"I'm also Angus's," Jack said with a smile.

"Of course you are," Angus said, settling his hand on Jack's shoulder. She couldn't help but smile. Jack was from Maggie's first marriage and Angus had adopted him.

There was a beat of silence and Anice looked at Maggie, who was staring at Brody as if he were a freak. Well, maybe not that badly, but she had yet to respond.

"Maggie?"

She shook her head. "Sorry. Woolgathering."

Jack stepped forward and held out his hand. She almost told Brody not to touch him. Jack's empathetic abilities were strong. He would see beneath Brody's surface to the man beneath. Why was she worried about that? Brody was a good man who had been so damned proper she was ready to scream.

Brody took Jack's hand and shook it. "It's very nice to meet you, Jack."

Jack's eyes widened, but he said nothing, only nodded. Curiouser and curiouser. She knew that Jack didn't always take well to strangers, but he rarely kept his mouth shut when he met them.

"Phoebe wanted to meet you, but she's a little tired today, so she's in bed," Callum said. "Let's go into the library."

"Do we have to?" Anice asked.

Brody patted her arm. "Doona worry, love. I'm the same way about my cousin Esme."

She wanted to argue, but when she turned toward him, he was smiling down at her. Dammit. Unlike any man in her long life, his smile left her dizzy. It always made her want to curl closer into his embrace and take comfort there.

Someone rudely cleared his throat. She looked back over to her family. She was betting it was Angus, the wanker.

"Okay, but you only get ten minutes."

The look Callum sent her way told Anice he wasn't happy with her comment, and he would definitely ignore her ultimatum. As everyone filed into the library, Anice held back with Brody…and apparently Jack.

"Doona worry, love. Your family isn't going to scare me off."

She opened her mouth to respond, but Jack interrupted her.

"There are two of you."

Anice blinked and looked down at Maggie and Angus's boy. "What?"

"There are two of you," he said again, but he wasn't looking at her. His gaze was focused on Brody.

"Yes, there are. It's Anice and me."

The little boy shook his head. "No. I mean, that there are two of *you*." He frowned. "I don't understand it."

Something quivered in her belly. "What are you talking about?"

Jack looked at her, then back to Brody. "Never mind."

Then he hurried off to the library.

"What the bloody hell was that about?" she said to no one in particular.

Brody apparently thought she was talking to him. "I've no idea but I'm sure he'll tell us in time."

She cut him a glance. He was smiling at her, again.

Dammit, every time he did that, she couldn't think straight. She pushed those thoughts aside and led him into the library. It was better to get this over with sooner rather than later. Besides, she had plans for the night and nothing was going to get in her way.

***

THE MOMENT they stepped into the library, Brody wanted to curse. Jack was sitting on one of the sofas. At the moment, it was the only place left for him to sit with Anice.

Bugger all these creatures.

Shut up.

He walked over and waited for Anice to sit down next to Jack and then he sat on the other side of her. Jack leaned forward and looked him. Brody didn't know what that was all about, but the boy smiled at him. He smiled back. Something shifted in Jack's demeanor and he relaxed. Whatever he was worried about, the boy apparently worked it out. Good, because if any of the Lennons knew what he was, or what he was up to, they would definitely kill him.

"Good, now that we're all here, I would like to know what the hell we are doing here? I mean, I can't remember there *ever* being a time when we dragged one of your women in here and asked them questions."

Okay, so Anice was going to take the militant view right now.

"Anice," Callum said, his voice filled with humor and irritation.

"I have to agree with Anice here," the witch called

Meghan said. Granted, most people didn't know she was a witch, but he did. They could always sense their own kind. The fact that she hadn't said anything told him he had cloaked his abilities well. Maggie was another matter.

She kept staring at him as if trying to figure out a puzzle. He glanced down at her son. He was gazing at him with the same look. This was getting a little too weird.

"What I want to know is why we are having a meeting about my date?" Anice demanded. Her anger vibrated through her entire body and reached out to him. He had never had such a strong connection to someone he wasn't blood related to.

Smack them down for questioning our mate.

Settle down.

He barely held back the growl that rumbled in his chest.

Anice glanced over at him as if she heard it, but he was sure he had suppressed. If he was in tune with her, there was a good chance that she did. Mates could read each other's thoughts. The closer the relationship, the more the mate felt and heard.

"We just wanted to get to know Brody better. I know we work with him, but it's different now that he's dating you. You understand," Callum said calmly. That said he was accustomed to Anice questioning him, which wasn't a bad thing. It meant that he respected his cousin.

Anice wasn't as accepting. Her frown turned darker, her indignation growing by the minute. Brody took her hand, stroking the top of it with his thumb. Callum followed the movement. Brody didn't care. His mate needed comfort, and he couldn't resist the primal urge to soothe her.

"It's all right, love. I can handle a little questioning. If I had a sister, I would be the same way."

Truth was, he did have a sister, but she was barely talking to him at the moment. She wasn't thrilled with this plan of his and refused to return from the Americas to help him. How she found Texas a good place to live was beyond him.

"We need to get going or we'll miss our reservation," she said.

He nodded. "True." He turned back to Callum. "I'm not sure what you planned on getting out of this, but I am more than happy to oblige, but I doona want to miss our reservation. It took a bit of luck to get a table at the Tower on a Friday night. I would be more than happy to return at another time to be interrogated."

"No, I will not have it," Anice said standing. "I didna question any of you with your relationships, and my new sister and cousins were not as well known to me as Brody is to you."

That's our mate.

Even though he agreed with his wolf, he definitely understood where the Lennon's were coming from.

"It's different because I'm dating you," Brody said, standing next to her.

"I have an idea. Come for dinner tomorrow night," Callum said. "Phoebe really wanted to meet you, but she was too exhausted tonight."

"Of course," he said, trying to keep his mind on the topic at hand. It was, however, a little difficult to do thanks to the woman beside him. Her own natural pheromones wafted over the air to him, and it was all he could do not to lean closer to take a sniff. That would definitely raise some concern with her family.

She opened her mouth to argue with him, but he stopped her with a smile. "Doona worry, love. Unless you're worried about having me here for a dinner."

He could tell everyone was watching, felt their gazes boring into them. He ignored everyone else because of the woman before him. She was his entire world at the moment.

"No, of course not," she said, her face flushing. "We should get going."

"Indeed," he said. "I look forward to meeting Phoebe tomorrow."

With that, they walked out of the library together.

"I'm really sorry about that," Anice said, embarrassment coloring her voice.

"No worries, love. I said it wasn't a problem," he said as he took her coat from butler. Belvidore gave Brody a strange look but he said nothing else. He helped Anice on with her coat, then she turned to face him.

"Let's not worry about your family, my family, or anything else. We have a table at the Tower, and I'm looking forward to spending a night with the most amazing woman I've ever met."

She studied his gaze for a moment longer, then her lips curved up into a smile. "Let's."

As he took her hand and walked out to his car, he hoped that he hadn't just made a big mistake. He hadn't been able to discover just what his cousin was up to, or why it was so important that he go after Anice. The truth was, from the moment he'd met her, he had been sure there was a connection between them.

CALLUM TRIED to tiptoe into his bedroom, but he should have known he couldn't get away with it.

"What happened?" Phoebe asked.

Their bedroom was dark, but with enough light from the moon outside for him to see her in the bed. As she turned to face him, his heart warmed. It was hard to believe he had lived over two hundred years before he found her. Now that he had her, he couldn't imagine living without Phoebe by his side.

"Everything is fine, love. You should be sleeping."

She reached over and turned on the light, then pulled herself up. The sheets fell away, resting on top of her massive belly. He was going to be a father in a matter of weeks. It boggled the mind. He had never thought to be one, not after a couple of centuries. Now he had the love of his life and a bairn on the way.

"Callum, please quit looking at my stomach like it's from the movie Aliens."

"I'm sorry, love, I was just thinking I never thought I would make it to this point. I never thought I would have a woman made just for me. Now, with this little one coming..."

She smiled. "I understand completely."

She shifted over and patted the mattress next to her. He did her bidding and sat down next to her.

"I was asleep, but my dreams are a little weird lately, and then the passage I worked on before I went to sleep has me worried."

He glanced at her table and saw the diary with a piece of paper sticking out. "Do you mind?"

"Go on."

He picked it up.

The one with two selves is the protector, the one who will always ensure the safety of the pack. He will do what is right for all those involved, even if he seems duplicitous. But fear not, for his love is true and his protection is strong.

"What the bloody hell does that mean?"

"I don't know and that's what has me worried. There are a lot of passages dealing with duplicity. Do you think that could have anything to do with the McWaltons?"

"They are indeed duplicitous, but I can't see that Gavin would change now. He's been easy going. I've yet to hear a peep from him or his nutty family since he took over."

She nodded. "The one thing that worries me is that this has something to do with Anice, I'm sure of it. What did you think of this Brody man?"

"He's a good worker, and he said he would come for dinner tomorrow night."

"Oh, good, then I can meet him."

"And Rena can meet him. She's better at reading thoughts."

She nodded. "Good. Anice likes him a lot."

"Yes, I know."

"And that worries you."

"There's only been one other time she seemed this infatuated."

"That was bad, and you think this would be bad."

"No." He sighed. "I guess so."

"Let me remind you that I had a horrible marriage."

"I know."

"But that doesn't mean I would pick badly my second time around, and indeed I did not. I believe you can agree with me, yes?"

He smiled. "Indeed."

"I know that all of you were hurt by her pain, by what she went through, but it seems that Anice has learned from it and moved on."

He sighed. "You weren't there, love."

"No, but I see a strong woman who has spent a century alone since the incident. She has recovered."

"Meaning?"

"You are more delicate than Anice."

"Excuse me?"

"She has moved passed the incident, but none of the men in the family have. You are definitely the weaker sex. And because of that, you need to learn to deal with it. Anice has a right to happiness, but I think that you and your cousins have kept her from achieving that."

"What the bloody hell do you mean?"

"That you four haven't dealt with the pain and the guilt you felt over the attack. So, the way you dealt with it was to keep her from being vulnerable again. Anice probably was happy to let you do that for a time, but she's ready to find her own happiness, and all four of you need to—how is it Meghan says it—grow a set."

He opened his mouth, then snapped it shut. As usual, she was probably right. They had all been hurt and, yes, for him the guilt and been painful. Fletcher had been hardest hit since they were twins.

"How did you get so smart, love?"

"My superior English genes."

He threw back his head and laughed.

"Now, go get washed up. I feel the need to snuggle tonight."

"Anything for you love."

He kissed her nose, then rose from the bed and went into the bathroom. As he washed his face, he thought about his worries. One thing he had learned over the last several years was that things were going to happen no matter what he or his cousins did. And maybe after over two centuries, they would be able to find a way to live with that fact.

Chapter Four

Dinner started out splendid. It was the only word that Anice could use to describe it. Brody had reserved one of the purple booths that usually sat four people, allowing them to sit together and look out the windows.

"I'm very impressed," she said as the waiter delivered their wine and salads.

Brody nodded the waiter away. "I thought we should celebrate."

"Indeed?"

"It's been four weeks since you asked me out."

She blinked. She knew it had been a month, but she didn't realize that it was the actually four-week mark. She lost track of the days and weeks. Again. She seemed to have lost the ability to keep track of the things going on outside of the family.

"You didn't realize it, did you?" he asked, a self-depreciating smile curving his lips.

"I'm sorry."

"No, doona be. You've had a lot going on with your family."

"What do you mean?"

"I would think any sibling would have a lot on their minds when the other is getting married, but a twin has to be even more so."

She sighed. "I love Rena like she's my sister. It's nice now that I finally have a better advantage against my brother and cousins after all these years."

"What do you mean?"

She dug into her salad. "Being the youngest, even by a few minutes, and female is a pain in a family of men like my cousins and brother. I respect them, but they are a bit overprotective, considering I've been taking care of myself for…years."

Damn. She almost let it slip that she had been taking care of herself for decades…centuries. Brody made it easy to forget herself, and she wanted to tell him the truth about her family. Every one of her cousins and her brother had found someone they could trust after years of being alone. Now, she wanted to find that person, and she thought it might be Brody. Still, something held her back. Revealing their secret could end in disaster, although she had no idea why.

"Understandable. You are not only beautiful and intelligent, you have a lot of money. It's hard to trust people."

She swallowed her bite of food and studied him. "You sound like you speak from experience."

"My family doesn't have the kind of money or power the Lennons do, but there are some…I guess you would call them artifacts that we hold dear. That along with the family lands, but we lost them years ago."

She saw the sadness in his gaze and felt it down to her soul. She knew what it was like not to have a home. They had a huge mansion, but it was not on McLennan land. In fact, none of them had stepped foot on McLennan land since they'd run to safety all those years earlier. They were so close to being able to do that if they could find the last stone.

"I understand that. In today's world, people doona take the family land seriously, but for many Scots, it is sacred. It seems that the remnants of the Clearances still linger today."

He smiled. "You sound like you would prefer Scottish independence."

"Yes. I see no reason not to be our own country."

He nodded and held up his wine glass. "I completely agree," he said, touching his glass to hers when she raised it.

Anice took a sip of wine and enjoyed the dark cherry and blackberry taste of the cabernet Brody had ordered. She sighed in pleasure.

"I take it you like the wine selection," Brody said.

"Yes." She glanced around at the people in the restaurant. It was still hard to get accustomed to having money, being able to go places like this. A century earlier, they had just decided to start working on their business, but they all had to sacrifice, especially through the world wars. Now, they had more money than they could ever hope for. "I've only been here once before, and it was for a work thing."

"I was told that this is a very impressive date place."

She focused on him again. She had thought it before and she would always think it. He was a pretty man. She didn't think she had ever seen a man with eye lashes as long as his. "Is that a fact?"

He offered her a quick smile, and she felt her heart do the little uptick as usual. She had it bad when just his smile was making her dizzy. Bloody hell, she knew that. She'd had it bad for him for the last few months.

"But my cousin, Esme. She feels that my brother and I are not very good at dating."

"I would say you are pretty good at it."

He leaned closer and brushed his mouth over hers. She felt the small gesture all the way to her toes. She was ready to say bugger all to the meal--which wasn't a common thing for her--and beg him to take her back to his bed. When she opened her eyes, she didn't find Brody looking at her. Instead, he was looking at something over her shoulder.

Brody pulled back slightly, but he stayed close by. Anice wasn't sure why.

She turned to see what caught his attention. Gavin McWalton stood only few feet away. Her first instinct was to run. Every laird of the McWaltons made her feel that way. It was as if some primal instinct told her that she was in danger. Fear wound through her even as she tried her best not to show it. She thought she heard a growl from beside her. She glanced at Brody, who was glaring at Gavin.

She looked back to Gavin. He didn't look as put together as he had when she ran into him last year. In fact, while anyone would say he was still attractive, there seemed to be something beneath the surface. She was sure other people probably didn't pick up on it, but she certainly had.

Gavin was a man who always dressed perfectly. His hair trimmed short, his clothes would be from the best shops and tailored.

That was not the man standing before them.

He looked a bit disheveled, as if he'd worn his clothes

to bed. His hair was longer than normal, and, well, looked a little dirty and unkempt. He hadn't shaven in at least a couple days. This wasn't the growing of a beard. It was just not keeping himself up. In other words, he was a bloody mess.

"Anice."

She nodded but didn't address him. She was still trying to work out that he was there, standing in front of them, scaring the hell out of her. Their run-in before had been...pleasant. She hadn't been scared of him until she realized who he was. It was different this time. The way he stared at her sent a sliver of cold fear curling in her belly. It took all of her control not to get up and run out of the restaurant. That and Brody had moved closer to her and had taken her hand. It wasn't that he was trying to trap her there. In fact, it felt as if he was trying to protect her.

"I didn't know that you knew each other," Gavin said, leaning against the table. The smell of whisky permeated the air. He was beyond pissed, and he didn't appear to be leaving any time soon.

"Brody works for Lennon."

He barely glanced at Brody, then focused back on her again. Sick amusement seemed to dance in his eyes. "Interesting."

"I doona know why it would be interesting to you."

An evil smile played about his mouth. "Because, who would have thought you would hire a McWalton to work for your company?"

The room around her shrunk away as her head started to spin.

She turned to face Brody, hoping that he would deny it. The anger and guilt were easy to see in his expression.

"Oh, I guess you didna know." He sighed. "I seem to

have stepped in it, so I'll leave you two alone. Please, doona hold it against him. I'm sure he is completely devoted to his job."

The warmth that had surrounded them evaporated with each word the bastard McWalton uttered. The waiter showed up with their meals and Gavin tipped his head in their direction.

"Have a wonderful evening."

With that he left, taking what joy she had been experiencing with him. She was sure that was his plan from the beginning, and she really hated that she allowed him to accomplish his task. As the waiter set their meals on the table, Anice took the time to pull herself together.

"So, you're related to that monster."

She didn't need him to say anything. She saw the guilt in his expression. Her heart sunk to her stomach, as a sense of hollowness filled her. Once more.

"I should have told you."

She cocked her head to one side. "You know of the issues we have with the McWaltons, but you still pursued me."

"I didn't exactly know."

Anger and pain twisted inside of her.

"You did, or you wouldn't have said what you just said." She closed her eyes trying her best not to cry. She had been duped once again by another McWalton. "I'm so bloody stupid," she whispered.

"You're not stupid," Brody said, his voice harder than she'd heard before. She opened her eyes and studied him for a long moment. He looked angry. At her? At being caught? Who cared? Not her. Well, she did, but at least she could still pretend not to.

"I call this date over."

She threw her napkin down. While she wanted to scream at him, along with kicking him under the table with her very pointy pumps, she couldn't. People knew she was the face of Lennon Industries.

"We'll get this boxed up, then we can go somewhere and talk."

"Nope. Not ever," she said, slipping on her coat, then sliding across the booth and rising.

"How do you plan on getting home?"

"I'm a big girl. I've been finding my way home for, well, a long time, as you know."

He opened his mouth to argue with her. Fear that he would convince her to stay, to make her see that he wasn't all that bad—even though she knew he was—had her backing away from him.

"Anice, love—"

She leaned down and grabbed the knife by his plate. She held it there on the table with the pointy end near him. He looked down at the knife and swallowed as his gaze rose to hers. Anice took sick satisfaction that she had scared him, if only a little.

"Doona tempt me, you bastard. You have no right to call me love, *ever.*"

She dropped the knife and turned to leave the restaurant. She saw Gavin out of the corner of her eye. He was laughing at her...or both of them. She wasn't sure. Either way, she was done with this.

She clicked on her phone as she stepped out of the restaurant. Before she could make a call, she saw Belvidore parked across the street. Dammit, she didn't need her entire family knowing what went on. At least not tonight. She would have to tell them before dinner tomorrow night, but she didn't want to deal with the humiliation tonight. She slipped into the passenger seat of the sedan.

"How did you know?"

"Master Jack."

She nodded. The old family retainer and Jack had a special bond. "Who knows?"

"Jack. And, of course, me."

She glanced at him out of the corner of her eye as he took off from the curb. "You didna tell anyone else?"

"No. Jack swore me to secrecy. They will find out though, my lady."

She sighed and looked out the window. "At least for tonight, I want to pretend that nothing happened."

"It is a lady's prerogative."

"Indeed. What all did he tell you?"

"Only that you would need a ride home tonight. He was worried for your safety. He also said to prepare for a visitor tonight."

Anice turned from the window and looked at him. "What?"

"He said that your mate would follow. Something about he has no choice in the matter."

"Jack has no choice?"

"No. Mr. Stewart."

She frowned. "If he does, I might just use that bloody sword and whittle away his favorite bits and pieces."

"Again, that would be your prerogative."

She chuckled at first, then a sob caught her unaware.

"My lady," Belvidore said, his voice filled with embarrassment.

She pulled herself back from the edge—barely. When she had her emotions under control, she said, "Doona worry, Belvidore. Just drive me home. I'll try to keep it together until I get to my room."

He drove along in silence for a few minutes, then said, "He doesna deserve you, my lady."

She nodded but said nothing else as Edinburgh disappeared from view and the darkness of the night filled her vision. She would eat chocolate and possibly drink an entire bottle of wine by herself. As Belvidore said, it was her prerogative.

ONCE BRODY PAID THE CHECK, he grabbed the two containers of food and started toward the door. Why he got the food, he had no idea. It felt a little silly, but the waiter had boxed up the food, and Brody couldn't just leave it there on the table.

He felt the study of just about everyone in the restaurant. A few people who were just curious, but he knew many of them knew who Anice was. Her family spent a fortune in the town and employed a lot of people. Add in that she was the PR person for the company, well, that made it worse.

He saw his cousin from the corner of his eye, and turned to face him in the reception area of the restaurant.

"What the bloody hell do you want?"

Kill him now. He needs to be gone.

His wolf was right. Gavin needed to die, but Brody couldn't risk a fight in public. His wolf clawed at his control, trying to come out. That would be disastrous for not only him, but every shifter in Scotland.

"So sorry, cousin," he said, the sick amusement he had heard earlier in his voice was still there.

A growl vibrated through his entire body. His wolf wasn't happy.

"This was your plan all along, wasn't it? You tried to get her interested in you, and she rebuffed you. Yeah, I see it now. So, you decided to humiliate her."

"And you. Doona forget that. Of course, your kind always should be humiliated."

Now. Maim him now.

No. Not yet.

An angry snarl was the only response he got from his wolf. Dammit. His brother had been right. Hell, Brody had been worried about the situation and why Gavin had wanted Brody involved.

"Right. Understand that if you come close to Anice ever again, you will regret it."

"Oh, Beta Boy, I would never be afraid of you."

He stepped closer and allowed his wolf to come closer to the surface. He shivered with the need to hurt his cousin. Gavin's smile faded.

"What about Cayden?"

"What?" he said, his face blanching.

"Or maybe you'd like to go up against Esme?" When Gavin didn't respond, Brody nodded. "I doona come on my own, but your kind would never understand that. We stand together. Always. Remember that next time you think to fuck with one of us."

Brody didn't wait for an answer. The moment he stepped out of the restaurant, his brother and Esme were there. Anger permeated the air. Most of it was from his brother. Brody could feel it course through Cayden. As Alpha, he would want to exact revenge. It was part of not only his character, but his chemistry. The Alpha of every pack wanted to protect, to be the one who ensured the safety of everyone.

His cousin Esme was furious. Her dark hair was uncovered; although, she wore one of her favorite robes. Anger darkened her blue eyes. When Esme got mad, people tended to end up bloody. He wanted to sic her on Gavin, but getting to Anice was most important. She was probably already home.

"Thanks for coming."

He had called them the moment Anice had walked out of the restaurant. He knew he would need backup, just in case Gavin went completely nutters and attacked him.

"Of course. Can I turn him into a toad?" Esme asked, looking over his shoulder. Brody glanced back to see Gavin standing inside, like the coward that he was.

"Not just yet. I have to get to Anice."

While Brody was angry, he was in pain also. Every emotion she felt coursed through him. Her pain was starting to become his, and they had not as yet mated. Damn.

"I think you should give her a day or two," Esme said.

"No," Cayden said, answering for him. "Now that Gavin has shown his hand, she's definitely in danger. Let's go to their place."

Tell our Alpha to shove it.

"I can handle this on my own."

"No. You can't. You connected to her more than you admitted to me." He opened his mouth to argue with his brother, but Cayden held up a hand. "Doona lie to me. We doona have time."

"I can handle it."

"No. You can't. Your mind is going to be on Anice.

Right now, at least, they doona know about us, and it would be best if we kept it that way. You need backup. Hopefully, her brother doesn't castrate you."

He nodded. "Let's go."

He followed his brother and Esme to Cayden's SUV. As they drove through the streets, rain started to fall. He knew Anice was angry with him and he didn't blame her. That didn't bother him. It was the pain he had seen in her eyes that had hit him hardest. When she had whispered about her stupidity, he had felt her pain, her despair...and he had lashed out. It was his fault that this happened, and he would fix it.

He just hoped that none of those witches or immortals were set on killing him when he arrived.

Chapter Five

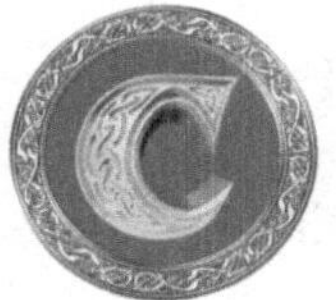

Anice was happy that she'd made it to her room without running into anyone. She wanted to do nothing more than wallow in pain. It was her right, at least for a few hours. She would normally think of lying to her family, but there were other issues with the bastard who had lied to her. He worked for them.

That would cause more problems. Did he get hired on with the company in order to spy on them?

Who knew? She definitely didn't. He probably did. And that was even worse. He had come into their public lives. Now there would be more questions, more worries. More humiliation. Not just within her family. Everyone at work would know that he had been hired to seduce her. And in the end, she remained a virgin. Bloody hell, she couldn't even do *that* right.

She stood in the middle of her room and realized she hadn't grabbed any chocolate on her way upstairs. She needed it. That and wine. Although, she didn't want to run into anyone. Not yet.

She walked over to her bed and sunk down on the mattress. Bloody hell, what a mess. The tears that she had been holding back started to fall from her eyes. She would never find happiness. It was as if she were marked. Or cursed. She snorted, and a fresh wave of tears flooded her eyes and trickled down her cheeks. What the bloody hell was she going to do? How would she ever be able to deal with all of this *and* find the amethyst? Everyone knew it was her quest, but while everyone else had a counterpart to help, she had to go it alone. Top it off that Gavin seemed to have lost his bloody mind and was most likely going to start causing trouble once again.

A knock at the door interrupted her pity party. She frowned, irritated and embarrassed. She didn't want to deal with anyone else tonight. She shouldn't have to. Her heart was broken, and she hadn't even had chocolate yet. Or wine.

Another knock.

"Aunt Anice, it's Jack."

She sighed and wiped her eyes as she walked to her door. She found him standing there, wearing his plaid PJs.

"What are you doing here, Jack?"

"I need to talk to you. I wanted to talk to Aunt Phoebe, but she's so tired these days, and I didn't want to tell anyone else. I have information about Brody."

"Yes, I know. He's the enemy."

His eyes widened, then he shook his head. "No, that's not it. Can I come in?"

She wanted to refuse. Didn't she have the right to wallow? Isn't that what movies tell her? She had a right to chocolate, wine, and bad decisions.

"Please," he deplored.

With a sigh, Anice stepped back to allow the boy to come in, then shut the door.

"What is it, Jack?"

"I'm sorry you were crying. It will all be better soon."

"I doubt that, but okay." He climbed up on her bed, then sat there and smiled at her. It was hard to believe this boy hadn't been a member of their family for very long. Now, though, she felt so blessed he was in their lives. Well, most of the time she did. Right now…she wasn't so sure. "What is it about Brody?"

"He's your mate."

Then he smiled. He said nothing else, but he was looking at her as if he had revealed the hidden truths of the universe.

She blinked. "What?"

"I'm not sure what it means, but I just kept hearing that you were his mate and that the other person in him wants him to just ignore everyone else and declare for you."

This boy always talked in riddles and most of the time it amused her. Not tonight. Not when she had been humiliated in front of the elite of Edinburgh. And, still, no chocolate or wine.

"The humiliation was important. It needed to happen."

Great. Just what she needed. A pint-sized truth teller. "God, you're as bad as Rena."

"What?"

"Nothing. What do you mean his other person?"

He shrugged. "Not sure, but there is another person within him. He talks to it in his head."

Great. Maybe Gavin had done her a favor. Brody

apparently had another personality he talked to. She only attracted bastards and people with mental health issues, apparently.

"It's not a personality. It's another part of him."

She blinked. "What?"

He ignored her question. "I'm telling you this because they are coming."

"They?" she asked as panic hit her in the chest. "You mean Gavin and Brody?"

"No. Brody and his family."

She opened her mouth to ask another question, but Jack stopped her. He grabbed her hand and started to tug her toward the door. "Come on. They're almost here. We need them. We can't win without them."

Dumfounded, she followed, stumbling behind him. As soon as they started down the staircase, there was a knock at the front door and someone rang the doorbell at the same time.

"Just who the bloody hell is that?" Angus asked stepping out of his bedroom. He saw his son with Anice. "And what the bloody hell are you two doing?"

"They are here. They will help us," Jack said as he continued down the stairs. By the time they reached the bottom, everyone had been roused and Belvidore was at the front door.

"Open it, Belvidore. It's them," Jack shouted.

"Of course, Master Jack," he said, going to do Jack's bidding.

When he opened the door, Brody stood there, drenched with rain, along with another man, who had to be his brother. A woman stood to his right.

"What the bloody hell are you doing here, Brody? Go away."

Jack threw her an irritated look. It was filled with such disgust, Anice would have laughed if she hadn't been in so much pain looking at Brody. He looked miserable and she should be glad for it. But there was that part of her that still cared. It was a big idgit part of her that needed to shut the hell up.

Wonderful. Now she was talking about another part of herself.

"What the bloody hell is going on?" Callum asked, as he stepped forward to stand beside her.

"Nothing. Brody and his family are leaving," she said.

The frown that Brody had been sporting turned darker. "No. I'm not leaving."

"He must stay," Jack said.

"No. He must leave. He's also fired."

Callum glanced at her, his gaze penetrating. "What did he do to you, love?"

"Yeah," Fletcher said as he stepped up beside her. "Tell us what he did and how many pieces we get to rip off the bastard."

"I think that we all need to calm down," Angus said. "We need to know what happened."

Good God, the man was always trying to soothe everyone. She didn't want to admit what had happened, what Brody was. Not yet. Instead, she wanted to hide away. Of course, that didn't happen because she was Anice McLennan. Nothing ever came easy. She felt Fletcher brush his arm against hers. The show of solidarity almost broke her. She would have broken if Brody hadn't been there. She refused to let him know she was breaking.

"What's going on down there?" Phoebe called out.

"There seems to be an issue with Brody Stewart. Now

we have to kill him," Fletcher called up. Someone laughed. Anice was sure it was Logan.

"You will back down," Brody's brother said. He didn't yell, as was the McLennan way. Instead, he gave the order quietly. The menace in his tone could not be ignored though. He looked so much like his brother, but much more dangerous. One thin scar marred his face, but didn't truly detract from his attractiveness. Still, Brody was much more attractive, in her opinion.

Dammit, there she went again.

"I think you need to reassess whose house you broke into," Callum said.

"Bloody hell," the woman said finally. She stepped forward and slipped off the hood of her cape and Anice almost gasped. Long black hair tumbled down the woman's back, and there was an air of magick around her. She reminded her of...she looked down at Jack who nodded. She was a lot like Maggie.

"We didn't break in. This very nice gentleman let us in. Thank you, by the way," she said smiling at Belvidore. The butler actually blushed.

"Is someone going to help me down the stairs?"

"Go back to bed and rest," Callum ordered.

"If you think you can order me around Callum McLennan, you are mistaken. I'm going to start walking down these stairs by myself, and since I can't see my toes, it is a little dangerous."

"Everyone, my office," Callum growled as he stalked off to walk up the stairs to retrieve his wife. They all filed into the room, Anice avoiding Brody, but he didn't take the hint. He walked in and stood right beside her. She side-stepped. He followed her. He didn't touch her, but he seemed to want to be near her. And dammit, for some reason, she was soothed by his presence. What the bloody hell was wrong with her?

Callum and Phoebe walked into the room. He led her to his desk, letting her sit in the chair as he stood beside her.

He leveled his gaze at Anice. "Explain to me what is going on."

She opened her mouth, but Phoebe took pity on her.

"I think we need to know who the newcomers are, love," she said.

Callum nodded. "Brody is the one with the beard."

"And this is my brother Cayden and my cousin Esme," Brody said.

"She's like Mommy," Jack announced.

Maggie looked at her son. "What?"

"She's a witch like you, but not exactly like you. She's like Brody."

"Of course she's like me. I'm her cousin," Brody said gently. She didn't want her heart to soften, but it did. Not a lot of people could keep their cool when everyone in the room was glaring at them, and especially when trying to understand a unique boy like Jack.

Jack rolled his eyes and Anice found her first smile since the restaurant. "I know that. I mean there are two of her."

"They are also McWaltons," Anice blurted out.

Her brother and her cousins growled, but Callum was the one who spoke.

"You're part of that bastard's family? You're right, Anice. He's fired."

"Callum," Phoebe said. "You need to calm down."

"Bloody hell, woman, doona tell me what to do."

"I've told you not to yell at me. Maggie will turn you into a goat."

"I will?" Maggie asked. "Why a goat?"

"Because he's stubborn."

"Why not a donkey?" Meghan asked with a laugh.

"Stop it. We are not going to go down this road. They are McWaltons. They are not to be trusted," Fletcher said, approaching Brody. "I get first punch at the bastard."

It was exactly what she wanted. She wanted her honor defended and for Brody to be hurt. Still, she had to fight the urge to step in front of Brody to protect him. She should hate him, but instead, she was ready to protect him.

"Fletcher, stop," Rena said. "Let's hear what they have to say for themselves."

"Thank you," Brody said.

"Then you can kill him," Rena said.

Brody glanced at Anice and she shrugged. "Rena is a little bloodthirsty."

"You can't kill them," Jack said, his expression turning pensive.

"I'm sorry poppet. I didn't mean that I would, it's just I doona like he hurt and lied to Anice," Rena said.

"But you can't hurt him because we need him. And his brother and Esme."

"What are you saying?" Angus asked. Maggie went down on her knees in front of her son.

"Tell me, love."

"We need them to defeat Gavin. He's playing with dark forces. They are coming for us, and if Brody and his family are not here, the rest of us will die."

"Love—"

"I know Daddy and his cousins and brother can't die. I

know they will live. But we can die, and Phoebe's baby. All of us will die." He looked over at Anice, his eyes filling with tears. "If you don't work with him on the amethyst, all of us will perish and you will never be able to break the curse."

Chapter Six

B rody's wolf prowled around inside of him, raising his agitation with each passing minute. He had to fight the need to pace around the office, but he couldn't. First, he didn't want to show his hand. He was nervous, but he was more anxious. Now that he was there next to Anice, he wanted to declare for her.

Do it.

He bit back a growl. Every primal instinct he had was fighting to be heard. All of them told him he should be taking Anice to a room and making her his mate. He rolled his shoulders as his cock twitched. Brilliant. He didn't need to get hot and heavy for Anice in a room full of her male relatives who wanted to kill him.

The other reason he couldn't prowl around was that there were so many bloody McLennans in the room that there wasn't enough space. Hell, he wanted to shift and go for a good hard run, but he knew it would freak people out.

"So, Jack, tell us what you mean?" Callum asked. He was the one Brody worried about the least, but that wasn't saying much. All of Anice's family looked like they wanted to kill him, especially her brother. Fletcher was ready to tear him apart. He knew, because he would feel the same way about his sister

Jack approached Callum's desk. "He needs to help Anice. And we need Cayden and Esme. They will help us fight off the bad man."

"Indeed?" Callum asked.

"We don't even know where the jewel is, right?" Angus asked.

"Well, I did get a lead," Maggie said.

"You did?" Anice asked.

"When?" Angus asked.

"What bloody jewel?" Esme asked. It was just like Esme to cut to the chase. She didn't like wasting time.

In mass, the entire clan turned toward her.

"Excuse me?" Angus asked.

"What jewel? Do you know what they are talking about, Brody?" she asked.

He looked at all of them and shook his head. "I'm confused by most of this discussion."

Callum blinked. "What do you mean?"

Cayden stepped forward. "We are completely confused by all of this. We can tell you what we know and why Brody was doing Gavin's bidding, but we need to know what the hell everyone is talking about."

Anice shifted beside him, he turned to face her. "You really don't know?"

He shook his head.

"Tell us," Callum demanded.

Brody nodded to Cayden and let him do the speaking. It was the way the family was. Their pack life was very structured. Alpha's normally did the talking, and

Brody was happy for it. He would never be happy as Alpha.

"Gavin is a distant cousin, who knows we want to gain our family land back. He has some money of his own--"

"Which he is sinking into something that is bankrupting him now," Esme said.

Cayden tossed her an aggrieved look.

She shrugged. "Hey, we all know he's gone batty. Which he has. He was normal. Well, as normal as the bunch of idiots can get."

"Esme," Cayden said.

She sniffed in Cayden's direction and crossed her arms across her chest but allowed his brother to continue.

"He promised us the lands if Brody here would get to know Anice. We didn't know the reason."

"So you seduced my sister in hopes of getting closer," Fletcher growled.

"No, I did not. No matter how much..." he realized he was about to admit that Anice had pursued him. Dammit. He didn't need to say something like that in front of her family. She apparently knew exactly what he had been about to say, as her face pinkened.

"I did not seduce your sister."

"You were going to say something else."

He shook his head. "Never mind. Not important."

"I need to know what Gavin wanted," Callum said.

"He wanted to humiliate Anice. We have no idea why, and it was one reason I advised against the idea. But Brody was already...dating Anice by then."

His brother knew that she was his soulmate. There was no way for his Alpha not to know, especially since the pull for him was so intense.

"But you did anyway," Anice stated, her voice filled

with sadness, and he wanted to kick himself, then go beat the shit out of Gavin. His mate didn't need to feel shame. She should be standing up to him.

"I couldn't resist."

She sighed but said nothing else. Still, he felt her shift further away from him emotionally. It felt like a dagger to his heart, but he couldn't deal with that at the moment. They needed to work through this other mess, then they could fix them. They had to, or he might just give up the will to live.

Bloody hell, he sounded like a teen in the first throes of an infatuation.

"So, tell me what this jewel is?" Cayden asked.

A long moment of silence filled the office.

"Good God," Esme muttered. "Haven't you figured it out? The immortality. Jack there said it was to break the curse."

"You know we're immortal?" Callum asked.

"Well, we *are* distant relatives to the McWaltons, so yeah. I mean, we never had anything to do with them."

"Why not?" Phoebe asked.

"A few reasons. One is that they sold our family out," Cayden said. That was putting it mildly. Embarrassed they were related to shifters and witches, they had helped hunt down wolves, even knowing they were actually shifters and their family. It was through that they lost their family lands. "Also, there seems to be a long history of madness with their lairds. We just want to get our land back."

"And he promised you your lands back?" Callum asked. He heard the understanding in Callum's voice.

"That and not to bother our family again," Brody said.

"There's more of you?"

He nodded. "We have another brother who lives in London at the moment. Our sister lives and works in Texas though and doesn't want to come home. Our parents, several cousins, and various other relatives live in Ireland. They all want to come home."

"And home is Scotland," Callum said. "So, what was your plan?"

"What do you mean?"

"Gavin wanted you to become friendly with Anice."

"Yes."

"And?"

He glanced at Jack and a knowing look filled Callum's expression.

"But you didn't do that?" he asked.

Brody shook his head. He was not about to tell them that Anice had been testing his control every day. If Gavin hadn't shown up tonight, Brody was sure they would have ended up in bed together.

"Well, I have all I need for tonight."

"They need to move here," Jack insisted.

"What?" Callum asked.

"They need to move here. Safety in numbers," Jack said as if repeating something he had been told.

Callum studied the boy, then looked at Brody, Cayden, and Esme. "I normally wouldn't think it important, but Jack seems to think it is, and he is rarely wrong. We have plenty of room."

"No. I will not have it," Anice said. Of course she did.

"Why not?" Callum asked.

"You have to ask?" Pain permeated every syllable she spoke. He felt it to his core. Bile rose up to strangle him. Brody was just finding out exactly how bad mating could be. In truth, this was probably only a tenth of what he would feel once they consummated.

"I agree with Anice," Fletcher said.

Tell them to bugger off.

He ignored his wolf. He didn't need to fight him and the entire McLennan family.

"I don't," Phoebe said.

"What?" Anice asked.

"I'm sorry, Anice, but I think it would be best to have them here. If Gavin singled them out, he is going to come after them also. I doubt we will get them to leave Scotland."

"No bloody way," Cayden said.

"See. And while you are mad at Brody—and you have every right to be—we can't leave them to be attacked by that idiot." She leveled a look at Brody. "But hear me now, I will have Callum toss you out and not think twice about it if you even think of hurting her again."

I like this one.

He had to agree with his wolf, even though she was singling him out. He liked anyone who stood up for his mate. Phoebe was definitely the matriarch of this clan.

"What about the jewel?" Esme asked.

There was a beat of silence as everyone turned to look at Maggie. "We are looking for an amethyst. I know where it is."

"Ah." Esme turned and walked out of the room.

"Where the bloody hell is she going?" Callum asked.

"We don't try to figure out anything she does any more," Cayden said.

"Since she came into her powers at twelve, she's been kind of a pain," Brody said.

"I heard that. I can turn you into a toad or a goat or

worse, an Englishman," she said, walking back into the library. "So, the last jewel, the amethyst, is missing from the sword hanging in the hallway."

No one said anything and Anice groaned. "She figured it out in less than thirty minutes, so there is no need to deny it. Yes, we are looking for the last one."

"And you know where it is?" Brody asked Maggie.

She nodded. "I have a lead, but I was going to wait until tomorrow."

"Why?" Anice asked.

Maggie shot a look at her husband, who nodded.

"I have been tracking down all the info on the amethyst and found a little nugget of info about a week ago."

"And you waited this bloody long?" Anice asked.

"I wanted to be sure because it wasn't promising."

"Oh for the love of God, just tell us," Callum demanded.

She sighed, glancing first at Brody, then settling her gaze on Anice.

"I just confirmed tonight that Gavin McWalton is in possession of the amethyst."

Chapter Seven

Bright sun splashed across Anice's room, pulling her out of a restless slumber. Covering her face with her pillow, she frowned. She didn't want to get up and face the day. She wanted to bury herself in bed and eat the chocolate she'd been denied the previous evening.

She knew, without a doubt, her day would intrude just like last night. There were a million things that had to be done. And she didn't want to handle any of them. She wanted to pretend yesterday never happened. She couldn't though because their lives were taking another drastic change.

Today Brody and his family were moving in.

Well, not actually moving in. They were keeping their rented house but, temporarily, they were going to be staying in this house. Her embarrassment to being an idiot continued. In her face. Every. Bloody. Day.

She sighed and rose out of bed. She'd had a fitful sleep and her body felt it in every ache and pain. For as long as she could remember, when she was stressed, her body tended to feel as if she were coming down with the flu.

Still, today was the worst. In fact, she felt as if she should crawl back into bed. Again, not common for her.

She shook her head.

"I'm not a coward," she whispered, more to herself than anyone else. Mainly because she was in her room, alone as usual. She stepped into her bathroom and looked at herself in the mirror. She was a mess. Her hair looked like it had been in a windstorm. Her eyes were bloodshot. Bloody hell. She looked as bad as she felt.

"I can fix that," Rena said from her bedroom.

Anice opened the door and found her future sister-in-law sitting on her bed.

"I'm not in the mood this morning, Rena."

"Yes, I can see that. Do you want me to ease the pain? I can."

"A shower will work."

Rena popped up off the bed and approached her. When she was within ten feet she abruptly stopped.

"There's something wrong."

"Yes, my nightmare is coming true. Another McWalton is moving in and I will have to live with my embarrassment in front of his entire family."

"Not the entire family."

She snorted. "That makes it better."

"What I meant is there is something different about you. I didn't pick up on it yesterday."

"I've not had my coffee. I love you but please, stop with the riddles. Or at least until I have my shower and a cup of coffee."

"Okay. I will let you go. But thank me first."

"For what?"

"I kept your brother asleep, so he couldn't come in

here. He wanted to, and I thought his plan was absurd. Also, he wants to beat up your mate."

"Brody is not my mate."

She ignored Anice's comment. "He told me the plan last night. I was appalled that he wanted to show up here in the morning. His first thought was to comfort you, but I know Fletcher. It would have started out as comfort, then he would begin to rant about hurting Brody. I thought it might be a little too much for you."

Tears stung the backs of her eyes. She loved her brother, her twin, but he was as obtuse as their cousins. Sometimes a woman needed privacy. She stepped forward and hugged Rena.

"Thank you," she whispered. When she pulled back, Rena was staring at her with a look of confusion on her face. "Rena, are you okay?"

She nodded. "Yes. I need coffee myself. Do you want me to have Belvidore bring you a tray for breakfast?"

Another kind gesture. "No. I will have to face my family once again. No use hiding."

She nodded. "I'll leave you to your shower."

"Rena?"

She had one hand on the doorknob, but turned to look at Anice.

"Thank you."

She smiled. "I have to look out for you. You're my sister."

Then she was gone, slipping out of the room and shutting the door with an almost silent click.

Anice looked around her room. So many years she had spent living alone amongst her cousins. They would never understand. They had always found women to share a moment or two with. She knew Callum had a few longer-lasting relationships, and the others had too. She had not.

There had been a few flirtations and a few dates. She hadn't been ready to take a chance before Brody. A fresh wave of tears filled her eyes. Angrily she wiped them away. She would not allow people to think she was weak. And she would not cry in front of that man ever again.

With that resolve in her belly, she decided to start her day and get over herself.

BRODY STEPPED into the McLennan household and felt his wolf prance around.

I do not prance.

What the hell do you call it?

I call it being anxious. We need to be near our mate. She is so close.

So…prancing.

His wolf huffed, but didn't say anything else.

He had come ahead of his brother and Esme. His reasoning was that his things were packed and ready to go. The real reason was because he felt weak being away from Anice. It had taken a lot of control to force himself to leave in the early hours of the morning. By the time the sun had started to rise, Brody had been packed and ready to leave the rental he shared with his brother and Esme. Now that he was at the McLennans' house, he was barely able to contain his happiness. It was tinged with fever though, and not the good kind. Having his mate angry with him had left him a little under the weather. His head was pounding, and he was constantly switching from feeling cold to feeling hot.

Callum stepped out of his office and walked toward him. Today, he was much more put together. Not exactly dressed for the office, but definitely different than seeing him in pajamas. He wore a thick sweater and dress pants. He was shaven, but the night had worn on him too. Brody could see it in his face, and he could also feel the weariness that permeated the air surrounding Callum. The man had a lot on his shoulders and the worry about his child on the way.

"I see that you made it unscathed. Where is your brother and cousin?" Callum asked him.

"They are still packing up," he said.

"And you wanted to get here as soon as possible." He nodded. "Set your suitcase down there."

"I can take care of it."

"I know you can, but I want to talk with you. Privately."

Belvidore stepped into the hallway behind him. "I can take care of that, sir."

"I can--"

"Bloody hell just give him your suitcase. I don't have time for this."

With that, Callum turned and walked back into his office. Brody guessed that ended any discussion.

"He's a bit stressed at the moment," Belvidore said. "Otherwise he wouldn't be so rude."

"I can be rude. I'm laird," Callum's voice drifted out of the office. Belvidore just smiled.

Brody handed his suitcase to the servant and joined Callum. Anice's cousin was standing by the big window that looked out over the drive of the mansion...as well as the lands that surrounded it. He had his back to Brody, which told him that Callum either trusted him, or didn't realize that Brody could be a threat.

"Take a seat. Do you want a cup of coffee?"

"No, thank you."

Callum turned.

"I realize that we talked a bit about your involvement last night with Anice."

Brody didn't respond.

"I need to know what your intentions are."

He blinked. "I don't know what you mean."

"Good God, man. I need to know if you mean to stick with Anice."

"Oh. Is this where you warn me off?"

Take him down. We need Anice and if he stands in the way, he needs to be removed.

His wolf wasn't always so bloodthirsty, but waiting for him to consummate with Anice had left him a little batty.

"I have a feeling that ship has sailed," Callum said as he studied Brody.

He nodded.

"So, you have a lot of work ahead of you, but I don't want it to get in the way of our quest."

"It will not."

"Good. And know this: You don't really have to worry about me. True, I would happily castrate you if you hurt her again. But there are others you need to keep in mind."

"I know Fletcher is not happy with me."

"You think Fletcher is a threat?" He pursed his lips before taking another sip of coffee. "Well, I suppose he is, but he isn't the most vicious. You have two witches and a fae who would gladly torture you for fun. I would make sure to keep the three of them on your good side."

"Maggie and Meghan are witches, yes?"

He nodded.

That left Rena as the fae. They were scarier than anything he had ever encountered. Ruthless and deadly, they were said to have no real connection to emotions, but he didn't get that feeling from Rena.

"Do they have any connection to the diary?"

Callum stilled. "You know about it?"

"Rumors."

"From your cousin Gavin?"

"No. My family has a connection to it too."

"I knew it," Jack gasped from behind him.

He turned to find the little boy standing in the door-way. "Jack. What are you doing here?" Callum asked. "Where are your parents?"

"In bed."

Callum motioned toward the little boy. "So, you knew he was connected to your family?"

"We have to talk to Mommy about it," he said as he walked forward. "She will be able to tell you. It doesn't explain the two of you."

"Jack." Rena said joining them. "I've been looking for you."

"I came in here. Brody is family."

Her dark gaze settled on him. Odd. He was sure her eyes had been blue the night before. "Indeed?"

She stepped closer, then her eyes widened. It took her a second to tear her gaze away from him. She looked at Maggie's son. "Jack, you need to go eat."

"I want to stay here," he said.

"Master Jack," Belvidore said from the doorway. "Time for breakfast."

"You can come back in here as soon as you are done," Callum said.

"Okay. I want to talk to you about your family. Where is Esme?"

"On her way in a bit."

"Good. She and your brother need to be here."

He nodded. "They are coming, I swear."

The pensive expression transformed into a smile, and he looked more like the little boy he was.

He hurried out of the room, grabbing Belvidore's hand as he did. Once they were gone, Rena approached them.

"I think we have something else to discuss," Rena said.

"What now?" Callum asked. His aggravated tone almost made Brody smile. It couldn't be easy handling a family this big, along with a company that had offices all over the world. With the hunt to end the curse and a baby on the way, Callum had a lot on his plate.

"I think our friend here needs to explain himself."

"I did last night."

Rena slipped up on Callum's desk as if she owned the room.

"Hey," Callum complained. Rena ignored him. Brody had a feeling that she ignored a lot of things she didn't like.

"I didn't pick up on it until this morning when I was talking to Anice."

Our mate. Is she hurt? Does she need us?

"Anice? Is she okay?"

She smiled and nodded. "But maybe you want to explain why you don't want us to know your true nature?"

The room felt as if it were shifting around him, spinning out of control. *She knew.*

Good. About bloody time.

"What the bloody hell are you talking about, Rena?" Callum asked.

"Well, I thought we should know why Brody doesn't want us to know that he's a wolf."

Callum threw his hands up in the air. "Okay. Now you lost me, again."

Brody said nothing. His tongue stuck to the roof of his mouth as his entire body went on alert. That meant only one thing. He looked behind him to find Anice standing at the door.

"What?" Anice said.

Rena's gaze rose to Anice. Brody turned to face her.

Our mate.

She was gorgeous, but at the moment, there was a fragility to her that he was not accustomed to seeing. He knew it was there before, but she had kept it hidden under some very heavy armor. She was wearing a black sweater and jeans. She was bloody gorgeous.

And she is ours.

Not yet.

Not my fault, mate. All yours.

"What did you just say, Rena?" Anice asked.

"He's a wolf."

"I notice you aren't saying anything, Brody," Callum said.

"I cannot lie."

Anice snorted as she crossed her arms beneath her breasts. He couldn't help the wave of heat that slapped him in the face.

"Truly." He would never deny who he was unless it was to protect his family.

Why should you? We are superior.

Bloody hell, shut up.

"Brody?" Anice asked.

"Rena is telling the truth. The reason why Gavin has always looked down on my part of the family is that we are shifters."

"Shifters?" her voice was fainter and, if possible, her skin grew paler. He walked closer, worried she would pass out.

"Yes. We shift."

"Full moon and all that insanity?" she asked.

"No. We shift when we want to."

He said nothing else because he was afraid to. He was a coward. If she turned away from him at that moment, he wasn't sure he could survive the hit.

"No, they do not need to shift when the moon is full," Rena explained.

"Are you telling me we now have two witches, a faery, and a family of shifters living in our house? How did it happen that we attracted so many oddities?" Callum asked.

"You're immortal, so it's not like you're normal," Rena said with a laugh. "Phoebe is the only one who is truly normal."

"That doesn't bode well for whatever this conversation is," Phoebe said from the doorway. "Does someone want to explain to me what is going on?"

The mother-to-be radiated with hormones and, as it was in their culture, he was drawn to it. An expectant mother was to be protected at all costs, so he stepped forward to offer her a hand. Anice looked at him wide-eyed, but he ignored her. Instinct told him to be subservient to a family member in her condition. Babies were important to the pack.

He led her over to Callum, who stared at him as if he

had lost his mind. Brody waited until Phoebe sat down before returning to Anice's side.

"What the bloody hell was that?" Callum asked.

He didn't say anything because now that he stood next to Anice, he drew in her scent and was lost. He wanted to touch, to please, to capture her cries as she came.

"I'll explain since the wolf seems to be in heat," Rena said. "Shifters are very protective of the pack. While Phoebe isn't part of his pack by blood, she is important to Anice; therefore, he would lay down his life to protect she and her baby."

Phoebe blinked. "Wait, what? He's a shifter now?"

"We've always been shifters."

Phoebe sighed. "I would really like to delve into this, but I want everyone here. So, I need tea, something to eat, and we need to rouse the house. Something tells me everyone will have questions."

Chapter Eight

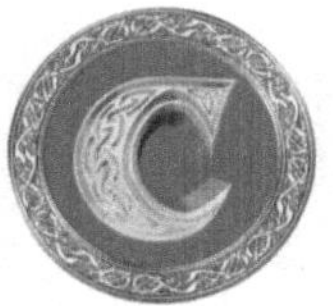

Anice sat down in the chair beside Brody's. She didn't think she wanted to see him today, let alone be near him, but the moment she knew he was in the house, she had been drawn to him. And no one had come to tell her that he was there. Instead, there was something inside of her, something in her soul, that had heralded his appearance.

The rest of her family had arrived, all of them called in for a family meeting. These were getting a little bit silly, in her opinion. They didn't need a family meeting to discuss Brody. He was going to help them with the jewel, that was all.

'So, now that everyone is here, tell us what is going on," Angus said.

"It seems that our new partners left something out of the discussion last night," Callum said. He was standing behind Phoebe, who sat at the desk, the diary in front of her.

"We didn't leave it out. It just never came up."

"Lame," Anice said.

Brody looked at her, sadness filling his gaze. Dammit, she wanted to pet him.

Where had that thought come from? She wasn't sure, but it was there, right in the tip of her thoughts. She wanted to reach up and stroke his jaw. She knew that it would soothe him.

"Okay, it was a little lame. My family not only has a connection to Maggie's and that diary," he said pointing to it, "but we're also shifters."

There was a beat of silence and Anice waited. With the McLennans, there was always an explosion after the calm.

"What the bloody hell are you blathering on about? Shifters?" Fletcher said, snorting. "Sure, you're a werewolf."

"You doona believe in shifters?" Rena asked.

Her brother looked at his fiancé. "There are shifters?"

Rena nodded. Then he looked back at Brody. "And your family? Esme and your brother, they're shifters too?"

He nodded. "Esme can shift, but she identifies with the witchy side of our family more."

"There are two of you," Maggie said.

"What?" Angus asked.

"There are two of you. It is what Jack kept saying. He sensed it. I thought maybe it was because you were lying to Anice."

"No. It's not like I hide it, but we doona announce ourselves around here. It could be a death sentence."

"That's why your family left Scotland. With the killing of the last wolves, you would be exposed," Maggie said.

He nodded. "Although many remain. To do that, you have to have your own land."

"Now it all makes sense," Phoebe said. Anice watched

Brody shift his attention to her cousin-in-law. "You need your land back, so you can return here."

"Yes. It is rightfully ours, but the bastard who now owns it keeps raising the price."

Everything clicked into place in that one moment. "Gavin holds your family's land?"

"Yes. He controls it all. We have enough money for what it would normally go for. But he has tripled the price. We know that even if we had the money, he would raise it above that price as well."

"And you have to be on your lands to shift?"

"No. My sister Eloise has told us she is never living in Scotland again. We moved when she was very young."

"She's the one in Texas?"

He nodded.

"But you want your land?"

"Yes, although we would take other land. Gavin has made that impossible."

"Sounds about right," Callum said. "That bastard would make sure no one would sell to you."

"Yes," Brody said, a grim look on his face. "He wanted to make sure we would do his bidding."

"We should be thankful," Phoebe said.

"Love?" Callum asked.

"If Gavin hadn't done that, I would have never been able to figure out that Anice and Brody need to go after the amethyst."

"You think he's supposed to be my partner?" Anice asked, even as she knew the reason. The universe had never been that fair to her. Of course he was the person she would work with.

"Yes. The passage I translated this morning has told me everything I needed to know."

Then she said nothing.

"Love, could you tell us?"

"Sorry," she said with a smile. "Pregnancy hormones are making me a little forgetful. Anyway, I translated this passage and now it makes even more sense." She opened the diary and pulled out a slip of paper. "The one with two selves is the protector to the key. He will ensure that she completes her quest. He will fight every enemy. His needs will complete her desires."

"What the bleeding hell does that mean?" Fletcher said.

"It means that the one with two selves—which is Brody, since we now know he's a wolf—is needed for Anice to complete her quest."

"What was all that blathering nonsense about desires?" Fletcher asked.

Anice loved her twin, but every now and then, she wanted to make him cry like a baby. Like right now. It took all of her control not to stand up and pull his hair. It was immature, but she couldn't help it. He was being an ass. As usual.

"The one thing that she has desired is to break the curse." Phoebe looked first at Anice, then shifted her gaze to Brody. "You need to stick close to Anice to keep her safe."

He sat up straighter and she almost wanted to groan. Phoebe had just given Brody the right to do what Anice was trying to avoid. Any time with him and she would make a fool of herself.

"No problem," he said, a smile playing about his lips.

She was doomed.

BRODY SETTLED IN HIS ROOM, trying to remember if he ever had a space this big to himself. He wasn't one who wanted to spread out. Most shifters, especially wolves, liked to stay close together. Safety in numbers, yes, but it was also a way of life, and being near other pack members was healthier for them.

Of course, he was much better off near Anice.

There was a knock on the door, then it opened.

Fletcher.

"Sure, come in."

Fletcher shut the door behind him and stalked toward him.

"I need to have a word with you."

He could see Anice there in his eyes, in his mouth. The two of them were twins and it wasn't hard to see. In personality, they were complete opposites. He knew Fletcher before he was even dating Anice, and they had always had a good working relationship. Now, though, he looked like he would happily castrate Brody.

"Stewart?"

"Sorry. I was just thinking how much you look like your sister." He shook his head. "What did you want to talk about?"

"You and I are going to go around about Anice."

He rocked back on his heels as he studied Fletcher. She had told Brody that Fletcher had come out minutes before her and had been trying to tell her what to do ever since.

"We are?"

"Other than working for the amethyst, you are not going to go near her."

He blinked. "Excuse me?"

Take him down. Teach him who is in control.

"Yes."

He moved toward Fletcher, using his wolf speed. Fletcher's eyes widened.

"I think you are mistaken. You doona control the situation. I do."

He didn't take a step back, Brody would give him that. He was either stupid, or brave—or both. At the moment, though, Fletcher might not understand the situation he was in.

"You control nothing," Fletcher said.

"I think you have that right," Anice said from behind her brother. He had been so intent on warning off her brother that he hadn't even noticed when she had joined them. That was stupid.

Fletcher made a face and Brody understood it. Anice wasn't easy to deal with. That's one of the reasons he loved her.

Brody blinked.

Love? No. They were mates, and while he knew there was affection there, it was more about their desires and compatibility with each other.

"Step aside, you idiot."

He didn't love her. She was bossy and would make a good mate for what was in store for them. Love meant that his emotions were involved and that was too damned scary.

"Fletcher."

He did his sister's biding. Anice was standing in the doorway. Anger lit her eyes and she had settled her hands on her hips. She was furious with both of them and damn if he didn't want her now.

Now.

"I think you need to leave," she said.

"Anice."

"Fletcher."

"This isn't over yet," Fletcher said, then he stopped by his sister and whispered something in her ear. She nodded, and he left after throwing another nasty look in Brody's direction.

When he left the door open, Anice rolled her eyes and shut it herself.

"You would think I'm fourteen years old and need to be taken care of."

"There's nothing wrong with the way he's watching out for you."

"Yes, there is. I'm a woman grown."

"One who fell for my line."

Her jaw flexed, telling him she was grinding her teeth.

"How kind of you to point that out, again."

Why had he done that?

Because you're an idiot. A coward.

Shut it.

"What is going on in your head?"

He opened his mouth, then snapped it shut.

Disappointment stamped her features. "Never mind."

"No. it's just...I was talking to my wolf."

"Your wolf?"

He nodded.

"That's a thing?"

"Yes. We have this other side of ourselves, one that drives a lot of our wants and needs. And they tend to talk to us."

"In your head. Like Jack said."

"Yes."

She nodded. Then silence. It stretched out until it was awkward.

"Is there anything else you want to know?"

She hesitated.

"Anything."

"You say you're a wolf and you can just shift." She snapped her fingers. "Like that?"

"Yes."

"Does it hurt?"

"A little. Nothing like the first time."

"So you aren't born like this?"

He shook his head. "Nope, normal humans until about the age of thirteen. Once puberty hits, we can shift."

She opened her mouth, then hesitated again. He hated she felt she didn't have a right to ask him anything. "I said anything."

"Do you only get involved with other wolves?"

"Apparently not, since I'm involved with you."

"We are not involved and that was because, well, we both know what that was for."

He opened his mouth to argue but she stopped him.

"No. I doona want any lies."

Tell her. Tell her about our feelings.

No.

"He's talking to you again?"

"Yes. I can't shut him up, especially around you."

"What's that mean?"

"He recognizes you as our mate."

"Our? Oh, I see, you and the wolf?"

He nodded.

"But I would think to marry, you would need another wolf."

"Not always."

"And you have one mate? Like there is only one person or shifter for you?"

"No. You have the potential for a lot of connections. Some are stronger than others."

"Stronger if you are both wolves?"

"Usually. Not with you."

She crossed her arms beneath her breasts. "I said doona lie."

"I'm not. I swear."

"Then explain yourself."

He drew in a deep breath trying to get his thoughts in order. He had screwed this up so much, he needed to ensure he didn't make it worse.

"From the moment I saw you in person, I felt a connection. I can't explain it because it's never happened with a human before. Not for me."

"But with me?"

"Yes. Then...when I talked to you, I couldn't get you out of my mind."

"That's called lust."

Tell her.

He ignored his wolf, who had started to pace inside of him, ready to pounce as he stepped closer to Anice.

"A bit. But not all. There is a connection between us. One that I truly doona understand yet."

I do, you wanker.

"I do. Your family has an obsession with me."

"I can't deny that. My cousin has lost his mind."

She opened her mouth, but there was a knock at the door.

"It's Callum. If either of you are naked, cover yourself."

Then the door opened without enough time for either of them to get dressed if they had been naked.

"If either one of us is naked?" Anice asked, irritated amusement filling her voice.

"Phoebe has something she wants to talk to you about. Both of you. Come."

Then he turned and walked out of the room.

"Does he do that a lot?" he asked.

She shrugged. "He's been laird, for over two hundred years. It's kind of who he is. I bet your brother isn't much better."

"No. He's been Alpha for about eighty years."

"So, you *do* live longer than humans?"

He nodded. "Our lifespan can be over two hundred years."

She opened her mouth to ask him another question, but Callum yelled out, "Come now or I'm going to be unhappy. Anice, let him know what happens when I'm unhappy."

A small smile played about her lips and her eyes twinkled. "He stomps around and mutters a lot."

"Anice!"

She winked at Brody, then she walked out of the room. And just like that, he realized he *was* in love with her.

Truly. Madly. Once in a lifetime love.

Bloody hell.

Chapter Nine

Anice followed her cousin into his bedroom, her heart worried and her head pounding. Her conversation with Brody hadn't made her feel any better. If anything, it made her even more confused. Feeling sorry for him and his family was understandable, but forgiving him was probably beyond her own abilities.

What was she thinking? Of course she had already started to forgive him. Well, not completely, but she understood his motivation.

Phoebe was sitting in a huge chair by the window. Her feet were propped up on an ottoman. Callum stood by her chair as if he were guarding her. The sweet picture they made together almost made Anice weep in envy.

Phoebe smiled at Anice.

"I thought…oh, there you are Brody. Come on in, you two."

Anice turned as Brody stepped up beside her. He looked…well, shocked.

"Are you okay?" she asked.

He glanced at her and nodded, then waved his hand

motioning for her to go first. She hesitated for a moment, then stepped in front of him. As she walked to the sitting area, he prowled behind her. There was no other word for it, and it wasn't because he was a wolf. She had thought that her brother and cousins all acted the same way around their women.

Dammit. She needed to stop thinking that way. She wasn't his woman and never would be. And why did that make her want to weep?

"Anice, are you all right?" Phoebe asked.

Anice blinked. "Yes."

"Good, now sit down," Phoebe said. "I'm sick of people towering over me," she said, giving her husband a pointed stare.

Callum waited until Anice and Brody had sat down before taking the chair next to hers. Anice had to bite her bottom lip to keep from laughing. She would have never expected Callum to be such a doting husband, but he was.

"I have found a few things that seem to make sense. Just so you know, Maggie, Meghan, and Rena are working on a plan to steal the amethyst. I am sure you two are going to have to deal with it, but we'll worry about that later."

"Steal the amethyst?" Brody asked.

"We haven't been able to buy them, that doesn't work," Callum said, his voice dripping with disgust. One thing they had excelled at was making money, but they found it completely useless in trying to gain a jewel. "We need to *acquire* them in some way."

"Yes. But what I wanted to talk about is Anice and the McWalton's fascination with her. I think I figured it out. Or, have an inkling as to why they may need you."

"Need me?" Anice asked.

"Yes. See, what I have been reading about is the *key*. I told you that earlier."

Anice nodded.

"Well, this passage today seems to indicate what I had thought was going on. *The Key is strong, and she is good. She will be the only one to unite the Clans, the only one who can save them all.*"

"Uh, what makes you think it's me?"

"It mentions you."

"What?"

"*Her mane is dark as the night and her eyes as clear as the sky above. She alone can bring them together.*"

She blinked. "That could be anyone."

Phoebe shook her head. "These books have nothing to do with any other family. It is just the McLennans and McWaltons. You seem to be the ones who they always talk about. I was confused at first because this baby is stealing my brain cells on a daily basis. I was trying to think of the reasons why the Clans had to be united, like all of the Clans of Scotland. But that's not what it is saying, or what Maggie's ancestors were saying."

"And mine," Brody said.

"Yes, and yours." She smiled. "But they were trying to say that the McLennans and the McWaltons needed to come together."

"Not bloody likely," Callum groused.

"Oh, shut it, Callum," Phoebe said with a smile

"You think we need to work with the McWaltons? How would that even work?"

"I don't think the witches meant Gavin or any of his predecessors. What I think they meant was the Stewarts."

She looked at Brody, who blinked.

"You think we are here to save you?" he asked.

"No. I think you are here to save Anice, and both of the Clans. You said it yourself. Every time one of them becomes laird, they go mad in some way."

"That is true," Anice said. "Remember, I ran into Gavin months ago. I thought he was just another well-dressed chap. A businessman. Now, he looks, well..."

"He's a bloody mess," Brody said. "He's unkempt. He can't seem to bathe. Although, I'm not sure if bathing would help. You might need to talk to Meghan and Maggie about this, or maybe Esme can help, but when you dabble in black arts, it tends to stain you."

"You mean your soul?" Anice asked, thinking back to the way Gavin had looked when he approached the table the other evening. He had been dirty, but Brody was right. It was as if there was some kind of stain on him. Just like most of his predecessors.

"Your soul, yes. But your soul starts to show on the outside. Unless you are truly a good witch, you doona know the spells to make it fade away and fool people."

"And they doona do that? They doona know magick?" Anice asked.

He shook his head. "They never minded being led around by dark magick or dabbling in it to get what they wanted, but they never learned the craft. Esme knows more about that than I do."

"I heard my name," Esme said as she stepped into the room.

"Esme," Brody said with the same tone her cousins used when they were embarrassed or irritated with her.

"What? You know if I'm distracted, I tend to wander. And this is one big, beautiful place to wander around in. So much coolness."

"She does wander. I should have warned you."

Phoebe smiled and shook her head. "No worries, love. Come in. You're family."

"No they aren't," Anice said.

"They're related to Maggie, which means they are part of our family," Phoebe said, patience and understanding threading her voice.

"Oh. Yeah."

For a second there, she had been thinking that Brody might be blood related and, well...that meant nothing because nothing was going to happen. Ever. Maybe.

Bloody hell.

"So, can you explain what Gavin is up to?" Phoebe asked Esme.

Brody's cousin sunk down on the carpet and crossed her legs. If the situation was weird, you couldn't tell by looking at Esme. She appeared completely at ease in the situation.

"Sure. All of them. That whole side of the tree needs to be burned down to the bloody ground, after being castrated without any drugs to help with the pain."

"I'm getting a little uncomfortable with how many times a day you threaten that, even if I doona like the McWaltons."

She rolled her eyes. "Get over it. They all deserve it. Their kind is infected."

"Infected?" Anice asked.

"With the curse."

She blinked and looked at Callum, who looked as confused as she was.

"We're cursed, not the McWaltons," Callum said.

"No. You are *all* cursed. Granted, while yours can suck because you've never had a normal life—and I assume there is something about babies born of immortals in the curse..." she waited for a nod from Phoebe before continuing. "Then it's nothing compared to the McWaltons. I mean, *they* set theirs in motion, not like you all."

"Okay, pregnancy hormones are doing a number on my brain. I'm confused," Phoebe said.

"Not just you, love," Callum said. "I've a feeling that both Anice and I are just as confused."

"Oh. Oh! Okay, so I thought you had worked all this out already. Anyway, the McWaltons were to leave you alone. There are probably passages in the diary about that, but maybe you haven't come across them yet. But from what my mum told me, the McWaltons could just go on their merry way and live. Meaning they had to leave your family alone. That was the one requirement. Easy, right? Not for those bastards. Of course, they had to ignore all the warnings."

"Esme," Brody said. "You're making my head spin and I'm accustomed to your rantings."

"I doona rant. I explain. Not my fault your stupid wolf brain can only handle some of what I say."

"We are both wolf and witch," he said chuckling.

Anice ignored the warmth that slipped through her at sound of it. She would not fall for a treacherous bastard who lied to her, even if they had to work together. She didn't care how much she wanted to.

Esme sniffed in his direction. "Fine. Let me say it easy for those witches without powers—"

"Sod off."

"And our lovely hosts," she said smiling in Anice's direction. Anice had to blink. Oh, lord. The woman was powerful. She hid it well, but it radiated out of her now, her eyes glowed and her skin shimmered.

This was one bloody powerful witch.

"So, you know about the initial curse, but my ancestors were kind of mischievous."

"They were arseholes," Brody said.

"Hey, you're related to them too, Brody. So, back to my story before the stupid wolf boy interrupted. When the McWaltons had the witch place the curse, they could have just gone on their merry way as I said. But witches aren't stupid. They understand human nature more than your average human."

"And she knew that the McWaltons would probably cause problems," Anice said.

"Exactly. There is some indication that my great, great nan could see ahead in time. Not all of us have that ability, but I'm guessing Jack does." She waited for a nod from Anice. "You know this."

"What do you mean?"

"I have a feeling they know you personally. That she knew you would be the one to connect everything."

"I still have no idea what that means. Phoebe just said I was the key to everything and now everyone acts like I should know something."

"Hey, I'm not the barmy witch who wrote the diary," Esme said.

"Witches," Phoebe said.

"What?" Esme asked.

"Witches. There are several different generations who have written this," Phoebe said.

"That makes sense. Even after marrying into the McWaltons, there was a good chance they were worried and only gave bits and pieces to write down."

"So they married into the family?" Anice asked.

"I'm not sure if it was a marriage of choice. The

McWaltons have always been devious. They were ruthless, but worse, they would sell their souls for power."

"And they have?"

Esme nodded. "So, my ancestors made sure there was a caveat on the curse. That there was a way out of it, and if the McWaltons tried to keep you from accomplishing the task, they would be ruined."

"They aren't ruined," Anice said.

"Answer me this: Do they have vast holdings? I know that Lennon Industries has a lot of money and power. What do the McWaltons have? And look how many of them have gone mad."

"Why do you think that is?" Callum asked.

"That they went mad? They dabbled in the dark arts. They must have gleaned from one of the witches, either through bribery or torture, that they were cursed in this way. To hold onto the curse against you, dark magick would have to be applied. They would never be able to make it this long. But it stains your soul"

"That's what Brody was just saying," Callum said.

"Yes. And that's why they get the way they do. They do the bidding, they use the power, but they have no idea how to handle it."

"What will stop that?" Phoebe asked.

Esme shrugged. "Unlike my very distant cousin Jack, I doona see the future. I do know that once you do claim your mortality back, there is an indication that their line will die out now that they have dabbled. It's why he's worried the most. He is the last of that side of the family."

"And if he can't produce an heir before we solve the curse? Then there will be no other McWaltons?"

"Well, there will be, but not from the original line.

That's why the baby is so precious and must be protected against all costs."

"That's why Brody was so protective of Phoebe," Anice said.

"What?"

"He walked her into the office and helped her sit down."

"We always protect the young," Brody said.

"It was more than that though," Anice said.

"Probably. More than likely, you will have to put up with both he and Cayden popping in to check on you. Their wolves will sense the danger, even if the human side of them does not."

"You say the baby is in danger. We've read that in the diary. We thought that if he or she is born before we solve the curse, that something could happen to the baby," Phoebe said.

"I doona know about that. I always thought the danger was from the McWaltons. They will do anything to keep that baby from being born, because they have no idea what it will be or what it means to them."

"What are you saying?" Callum demanded.

"That if I know McWaltons—and I do—Gavin is already plotting to kill Phoebe to prevent the birth of another McLennan."

Chapter Ten

Another family meeting was called, and it was just as loud and opinionated as the English Parliament. Of course, Brody didn't make that comment out loud. The McLennans might live in the modern world, but they held onto their old transgressions. It was hard to blame them. After the Clearances, they'd lost everything, including their family. He knew how devastating it had been to lose their family land, but at least the family had remained intact. Somewhat.

"So, this slimy bastard thinks he can just waltz in here and take Phoebe?" Angus asked. "Not going to happen."

The anger in his voice was understandable, but there was always a bubbling rage on the inside that Brody could sense. Angus was ready to erupt and that wasn't normal. He was known as being cool at work. He had never heard of Angus losing his temper, and Angus had been the one who appeared to be the calmest before this discussion. Now, Brody wasn't sure Angus wouldn't march into Edinburgh and kill Gavin with his bare hands.

"He thinks it, but it isn't going to happen, love," Maggie said gently. "We have wards up to protect."

"I can help strengthen them," Esme said. "I'm devilishly good at it."

"She is," Brody said.

"We'll take all the help we can get," Maggie said with a nod.

"Amen to that," Meghan said.

"Before you start that, I think we need to make sure whatever plan we have doesn't involve all of you," Anice said.

Brody was sitting next to her, thankfully. It calmed his wolf to be close enough to feel her body heat. Every second that passed meant that his wolf was prowling closer to the edge.

Because we need her.

"What do you mean?" Maggie asked.

He wasn't sure why, but Maggie was apparently in charge of stealing the jewel.

"Brody and I need to be the ones who grab that jewel, but I think we need at least two of you here, and I'm including Rena and Esme in that. For protection."

"I think we can handle Gavin," Fletcher said.

"I love you, brother, but no, you can't. We all know just how dark this magick can be. That line for the laird seems to be especially apt to lose their minds when they start dabbling. Leaving Phoebe unprotected is insane. If what Esme said is true, then we can't leave her alone. We need magickal people here to help."

Smart.

Of course she's smart. She's our mate.

She turned to look at him. "Do any more of your family know magick? Practice I mean?"

He couldn't answer. He knew what to say, but his brain just went completely blank. The words seemed to stutter in the back of his throat as he struggled to get them past his lips. Instead, there were flashes of them in bed together and the taste of her pleasure flooded his senses. His entire body went on alert.

"Brody?"

Thankfully, Cayden took pity on him and answered. "Our brother Archie practices. I can give him a ring and see if he can make it up here."

"I'll send the plane for him," Callum said.

Cayden nodded as he pulled out his mobile and walked out of the room.

"Okay, so the wards need to be strengthened first, then we will go over the plan with the two of you," Maggie said.

Anice turned away from him and his wolf growled. He bit it back, just barely. He needed Anice or he needed a good run. He didn't need to shift that often. Well, *need* was a strong word. They were half witch, and while most of them identified with their wolf more than their witchy side, it did give them an advantage. It took a bit off the edge. Almost all of them liked to shift, loved it in fact, but now it was imperative to shift. He needed to run off his lust for Anice.

"We have to be the ones who get the jewel, right? I mean, what are the chances that there'll be a gala or something like with Fletcher?"

"But there is. That's how I found out that he had the jewel. I'll talk to you about that when we get back," Maggie said.

"Maggie," Anice said. Impatience threaded through her and it snapped out at him. She might look calm and cool, but she was definitely chomping at the bit to take action. He could hardly blame her. They had been searching for this for centuries. They were so close.

"Protection is more important right now," Callum said.

Anice sighed and nodded, but Brody could feel her disappointment. It washed over him, and he couldn't help the need rising in him. He wanted to soothe her, make her feel whole.

You can do that and more…in your bed.

Bloody hell. His wolf was getting out of control.

Every moment he spent with her was making that wanker louder and louder in his head.

He felt himself leaning toward her, wanting to pull her closer to him or even up on his lap. Part of it was definitely sexual, but there was a deeper feeling of comfort. He needed to touch her to feel complete.

He drew in a deep breath and looked out the window. The sun was already setting, and he knew they were safe on McLennan land. He had a feeling that his idiot cousin wouldn't try anything tonight. Gavin wanted confrontation. He wanted to win by crushing not only Anice, but also Brody. So, until they went after the jewel, Gavin would sit back and wait. The barmy bastard was probably relishing the idea and fantasizing.

Speaking of fantasizing…

Damn.

He pulled himself back, with difficulty. "Is there anything else?"

Callum looked at him strangely. "We'll be eating in about an hour, so I guess we can go over the plan then."

He nodded. "I need to get out. I'll go along with the witches for protection."

Out of the corner of his eye, he saw Maggie open her mouth, but Esme shook her head. His cousin knew he needed to shift, and as fast as possible or he would make an ass out of himself and drag Anice to bed. Then she would humiliate him by kicking his arse.

"Good. I should be back by then."

He rose and followed the women out of the room. He met his brother making his way back into the office. He was still on the phone with their brother.

"Going to run?" Cayden asked.

Brody nodded. "Plus, I can ensure the safety of our cousins."

Maggie smiled at him when he included her.

"Meghan isn't related. She's a dirty American," Maggie said.

"Seriously, woman, I can make you bald-headed."

He ignored them and gave a pointed look at his brother, who nodded. "I'll make sure there are some clothes for you when you return. Back entrance. And, I will keep an eye on Anice."

He nodded and walked down the hallway, only to be stopped again. This time, it was by Jack.

"I want to see."

"What?" he asked.

"I want to see you shift."

He grabbed Brody's hand and dragged him to the end of the hallway to a side door.

"This would be best because there are bushes, and no one can see you naked."

He chuckled despite the raging need pulsing through his entire body. The boy had a way about him that was for sure.

Brody followed Jack out the side door and into the

garden. He was, indeed, correct. Of course he was. He probably knew every nook and cranny in the house.

"I will keep a look out so none of the ladies see you," Jack said earnestly.

Brody smiled. "Thank you."

Nudity didn't bother the Stewarts. Their kind didn't get embarrassed, even from a young age. Sexuality was natural and ensured the pack's survival. Still, he would never embarrass Jack. He was trying his best to be helpful.

"You won't eat me when you shift, right?" Jack asked.

"Of course not. I doona eat little boys."

He smiled, then motioned with his hands to tell Brody to get on with it. Jack turned his back to him and Brody started to disrobe.

"What do you look like?"

"I'll be the only wolf in front of you, so you aren't going to mistake me."

The boy giggled. It was hard to remember that he was a little boy. So many of the dire warnings came from him, and he always seemed so bloody serious.

Once he was naked. He allowed his wolf to take over. As his tendons lengthened and his bones cracked and reformed, he winced. It had been so long since he'd shifted, that it hurt a little more than it usually did for an adult shifter. Magic pulsed in the air around him as he felt his full coat of fur sprout over his body.

When he had finally shifted completely, Jack turned. His eyes widened. "Wow. That's so bloody cool."

Brody snorted as he laughed inside.

"Oh, no. Don't tell Mommy I said that, okay? She doesn't like me to use the word bloody."

Brody nodded. The door opened behind him and his cousin, Maggie, and Meghan joined them.

"Oh, my," Maggie said, crouching down to his level. "You are a pretty wolf."

Again, he snorted.

Pretty. What the bloody hell does that mean?

It means she finds us attractive, you idiot.

"May I pet him?" Meghan asked.

"Yes, you may. You can be a good boy, can't you?" Esme asked, amusement filling her voice.

He gave his cousin a look that let her know she would pay for that comment when he was back to his human form.

Meghan and Maggie ran their hands down his back and through his fur. Pleasure filled him. Not sexual, but of the connection he felt to them, especially Maggie. They were blood related, no matter how distant. It soothed his wolf and also his soul. Familial connections were important on both sides of his family.

That's great, but when do we get to run?

He motioned with his head to Esme, who gave him a devious smile before turning to the other women.

"He needs to run off some steam, doncha boy?"

Oh, he was going to get back at her, but he just nodded.

"Sounds good. We'll be near the house."

He nodded once again then took off, hoping that he could at least run off some of the need he felt for Anice. The cool night air rushed against his fur and he lost himself in the run.

Chapter Eleven

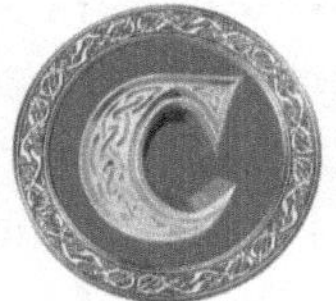

Anice was worried. Dinner had come and gone, and
Brody hadn't returned. As each minute ticked by,
she felt a responding click in her head. It grew louder and
louder. She shouldn't be this out of sorts, but Anice
couldn't seem to stop the restlessness crawling through
her.

To occupy herself, she'd offered to help clear the table,
but then the witches laughed and said they could take care
of the rest. At a loss of what to do, she started to walk the
hallways.

He hadn't been gone that long, and the witches had
assured her he was fine. Why did she feel so messed up
now that he was out on a run? It had been less than ninety
minutes and she felt as if she were jonesing for a drug.
The drug being Brody.

She stopped walking and rubbed her hands over her
face. What the bloody hell was wrong with her? She was
yearning for him, wanting to be near him at the same time
she wanted to smack him upside the head. More than

once. Then kiss him. It had seemed like forever since she had been able to kiss him.

Anice groaned, then pushed the thought aside. Instead, she focused on the present. She hadn't seen Cayden in a while, and she assumed that he had gone out after Brody or to run with him, or whatever they did. Irritated with her own thoughts, she grabbed her jacket and went to the side entrance. She stepped outside. The moon was bright enough for her to see the lay of the land easily. They didn't have a lot of lights that stayed on all night. They knew that there would be issues for the nocturnal animals that made the estate their home.

Just as she was thinking that, she heard someone behind her. She turned and watched as Cayden approached her. They looked so much alike, it still stunned Anice. Brody was probably about half an inch shorter than his brother, and his overall personality seemed lighter than Cayden's. There was the weight of being the leader on his shoulders. That and the faded scar. One long mark went from his forehead over his eye, then down to his chin. It was amazing that he hadn't lost his eye, with whatever had happened.

"He's okay, you know," he said in a gentle voice.

She nodded and crossed her arms. She didn't want to care, but she did. In fact, she felt anxious with him out in the wild. She glanced down and saw the clothes he was holding.

"Those are for him?"

He nodded. "He should be back soon."

They stood side-by-side for a long moment. She loved the night, always had, and now she was wondering why she had been so drawn to it. She remembered complaints from her mother that when she was a baby, she always preferred the night. And sneaking out of the house had been the one naughty thing she did. She couldn't seem to help herself. The night constantly called to her and resisting it had seemed impossible.

She glanced at Cayden. "You know, I doona need a protector."

He chuckled. "I know you are capable and, thanks to your witches and mine, you're safe. I know Brody would expect me to watch over you."

She groaned. "Doona start with that mate rubbish."

"It's true."

She glanced at him, then back out at the darkness. "Why didn't you need to run?"

"We doona need it as much as full shifters do. Our witch blood cools some of that. But Brody needed to run off energy."

"Run off energy?" When he said nothing, she looked at him. "What?"

"You're not *that* obtuse, Anice. I take it you haven't consummated?"

She felt her face heat. She knew she was a couple centuries old, and she shouldn't be embarrassed, but people didn't always speak in such plain terms. At least, not in front of her.

"No."

"Then that's why." He cocked his head to one side, then turned it to look out at the night. "He's back."

The thundering of feet against the earth filled the air around them. It sounded as if a large creature was rushing them from the fields. The air around them seemed to spark to life, snapping with light and energy.

"Doona worry. It's just Brody."

"Why is it so loud?" she asked, as the footsteps grew louder by the second.

"Because, he's your mate. You sense him, hear him more easily than others."

She scrubbed her hands over her face. "Bloody hell, I..."

Cayden touched her arm, but he froze when a growl rumbled. Anice opened her eyes to find the most gorgeous creature she had ever seen standing in front of her. There was no doubting this was a wolf, but she was pretty sure he was bigger than ordinary wolves. He was gray in color along his back but part of his snout and chest were white. Bits of red here and there, also black colored the fringes, along with his legs.

He snarled at his brother.

"Dial it back, brother," Cayden said, his voice harder than she had heard before. This was the Alpha of the Stewarts. Still, Brody snarled again, baring even more of his teeth.

Cayden dropped his hand. "Bloody hell, you wanker."

She had a feeling from Cayden's tone and his expression, that he wasn't accustomed to letting his brother win any argument. Brody calmed a bit, but when he approached them, he slipped between the two of them.

"I think my brother is a little jealous," Cayden said with a laugh.

Another snarl.

She reached out, then thought better of it.

"Go ahead," Cayden said.

She slipped her fingers through Brody's fur, and he shuddered in appreciation. When he looked up at her, she saw the man beneath all of it. In his eyes, the bright blue eyes, she saw Brody.

He growled, but this time, it sounded more like appreciation.

"Listen, while I doona have an issue with the two of you, I think he wants to shift."

She nodded, waiting.

"He's going to be completely naked and while I have a feeling he doesn't care, I do. I doona want to be standing with the two of you if he is suddenly naked…that's weird right now."

She opened her mouth to ask why it would be weird, because nudity didn't bother her, and she doubted it bothered Brody.

Cayden snorted. "Listen, I doona care what you do, but if he's naked and you're here, things could rise to the surface, if you get my drift."

She blinked, then chuckled. "Yes, of course. Sorry." She slipped her hand through Brody's fur once more, unable to resist, "I'll get going."

With that she stepped inside and found Esme waiting for her. "You knew I was out there?"

"I was hoping you would be. Brody is an attractive man, but he is a gorgeous wolf. Just doona tell him I said that."

Anice nodded and started walking, wanting to be alone with her thoughts. Of course, Esme followed right along.

"I wanted to talk to you about Brody. I know that you've softened a little bit, but just in case, I thought maybe we should chat about our boy. And yes, I call him a boy because the men in my family need to be knocked about a bit."

"I take it you weren't happy about the situation with Gavin."

"I hate that bunch. They burned one of my great aunts. Burned her alive. They have tortured others and got them to do their bidding."

"That's horrible. I'm sorry."

Esme's eyes softened. "Thank you. I'll make them pay and part of that is helping you and your band of idiot male relatives."

"Idiot males?" Cayden said. "Come now, you doona talk about me like that, do you?"

"Always. You deserve it."

He frowned. "You're being disrespectful. Again."

"You doona need to keep telling me. I know I am, and I really doona care."

Anice snorted and they turned toward her.

"Sorry, you just sound like I do with all of my male relatives."

"That's because they are lesser than us."

"Esme, could you pretend to be on our side?" Cayden asked.

Anice laughed, then something caught her eye. Brody had returned to human form, and was unfortunately dressed. Not unfortunately. He was dressed. Just dressed. She didn't want to see him naked. Not really.

"Oh, there you are," Esme said. "Come along. We have a jewel heist to work on."

"We'll be there in a second," Brody said.

Esme opened her mouth to say something, but this time, Cayden grabbed her arm and dragged her away. They continued to bicker but all she could seem to pay attention to was Brody.

His hair was a little wild and that made her think of slipping her fingers through his fur just moments before.

"I would really like to know what you are thinking at the moment."

She shook her head, as she felt her face heat up again.

"Oh, come now," he said, his brogue dancing over the words and sending a wave of heat slinking down her spine. "Doona leave me hanging, love."

"I'm not thinking anything you need to worry about," she said, her voice breathless. She needed to get away from him or she would forget herself and beg him to take her to bed. Before she could step away, he grabbed her by the wrist, then drew her closer. She didn't feel threatened. She knew without a doubt he would let her go if she insisted.

But she didn't. Instead, she let him tug her closer, then crowd her up against the wall. Her head started to spin with the wild scent of night air that seemed to cling to him. He studied her for a long moment and she thought he would kiss her. It wouldn't be that bad for him to take one little taste. He didn't kiss her though. He bent his head and nuzzled her neck. It was somehow more intimate to her. His tongue flitted out over her flesh, and she shivered. When she tried to swallow, she found her mouth too dry. What the bloody hell was he doing to her?

He growled against her neck. "So tasty. And you smell divine," he rasped out. Her own hunger doubled as she heard the need vibrating in his voice. She wanted to let go, let him take her right there against the wall. She deserved it, needed it. She had been through so much.

"Brody, quit flirting and get in here," Cayden yelled out.

It was the splash of cold water she needed to bring her back to sanity.

"We are not doing this," she said. She inwardly

cringed at her tone. There was no doubt if she couldn't convince herself, she wouldn't be able to convince Brody.

The smile he gave her told her he had every intention of trying to change her mind. Still, he said nothing. Instead, he stepped back and waved his hand as if to tell her he would follow her.

Anice tried to calm the butterflies in her stomach, but she found it beyond her ability. She needed to get away from him before she made an even bigger arse out of herself.

She walked down the hallway and he followed, catching up to her in two strides.

"So, do *you* think I'm pretty?" he asked.

Anice glanced at him. "What?"

"Maggie called my wolf pretty." He sounded full of himself.

"Maybe she has lower standards than I do. She *did* marry Angus."

Brody chuckled. "You *do* think I'm pretty."

She wanted to hip check him into the wall, but instead she had to laugh. His tone was playful, albeit still a little conceited. "Of course, you are pretty...as a wolf."

She felt a softening to him even when she knew she shouldn't. Just yesterday she had discovered his duplicity. Now, she was getting weak-kneed because his wolf was pretty.

She walked into the room and inwardly groaned. There were only two seats left, those on the loveseat. Of course, that's what she needed. Still, knowing that everyone was ready to get this meeting started, she took her place. Brody sat down next her, his smile telling her that he was definitely okay with the situation.

"You talked to your brother?" Callum asked Cayden.

He nodded. "He should be here in the morning."

"So, we have a few wolves, two witches, a faerie, and a bunch of immortals to help out with the situation," Callum said.

"I'm here to help," Phoebe said. "Just because I'm an ordinary mortal with no abilities, doesn't mean I can't help."

"Love, there is nothing ordinary about you," Callum said.

"And you have been more than helpful. If it wasn't for you, we wouldn't have four jewels and be ready to grab the last one," Anice said. "I found the way to break the curse, but you are the one who helped us get to where we are right now."

Everyone in the room, except the Stewarts, who were all still learning all the back story, nodded. Phoebe pulled out a hankie and dabbed her eyes. "That's the sweetest thing."

"Let's get this started," Callum said. Then, he took Phoebe's hand and urged her out of the chair. He sat down and pulled her onto his lap. The sweet gesture touched Anice's heart. Callum wasn't always the most demonstrative man, but he definitely had learned to show it around Phoebe. She had certainly softened those hard edges.

Maggie stood. "I will go over the plan in a bit, but I think we need to discuss who is staying here."

"Anice and Brody need to go to get the jewel so they're out. I think we can leave most of the magickal people here," Rena said.

"Why do we need that many people here?" Phoebe said.

"To protect you, love," Callum said. She opened her

mouth, but he stopped her. "And our bairn. We need people here to make sure the baby is safe. You know that."

"Okay. Sorry," she said.

Maggie smiled. "No worries. Now, the event that he's having night after tomorrow is designed for us. I can feel it. He knows we want that last jewel. He can say all he wants, or whatever he has said in the past, but he could have easily let us have the jewel as soon as he found it. He didn't. And he went out of his way to acquire it, if my sources are right."

"Your sources usually are," Meghan said.

"Just to be fair, he was normal last year," Anice said.

"What do you mean?" Maggie asked.

"I know what Anice is saying," Brody commented. "Even in the last couple of months, he seems to be a totally different person. That black magick..."

Maggie nodded in understanding. "Oh, right. Anyway, he's having a party and, of course, the slimy bastard invited us."

"He did?" Callum asked.

"Yes. So, I already RSVP'd for Anice and Brody. Angus and I will also attend."

"I thought the magickal people were staying here," Callum commented.

"I said most. From what Esme says, Brody doesn't practice."

"I would if I thought it would work, but I have little to no magickal ability."

"Except turning into a wolf," Anice said.

"Nothing magickal about that, love. It's the way we are born." What he said was totally normal, and his tone was a bit cocky, but normal. It was the way he was looking at her. Anice suddenly felt as if she were missing a red cape and basket of goodies for her grandmother.

Thankfully, Maggie saved her. "So, everyone else will stay here. I am contemplating what to do with Jack, as we think that Gavin will come after Phoebe and the baby then."

"This sounds too dangerous. To Phoebe," Anice said, glancing at the woman in question. "I doona want anything to happen to you."

"We doona have a choice. Not at this point," Maggie said. "We could send you away, but after talking to Callum and then to Esme, we thought it was useless. If Gavin wants to come after you, then, it doesna matter where you are. Familiar territory is the best bet. And if we wait to go after the jewel, she's still in peril."

She sighed. Brody reached out and stroked her hand. The small gesture calmed her a bit. "Okay. We know who is staying and who is going. What's the plan?"

Maggie smiled. "I get to do some straight up devilish magick." She rubbed her hands together. "I can't wait."

Chapter Twelve

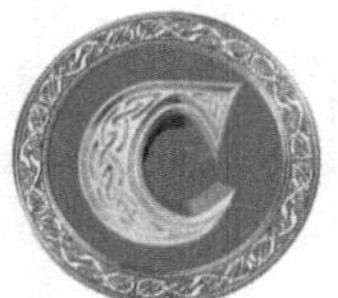

Gavin looked out over the night. Most of Edinburgh was still, the darkness cloaking the usual bustling city. As a child, he hated the nights. His father drank to compensate for his failures and tended to take it out on all of them, especially his mother. Now, though, he felt his soul ease every time the sun set.

He closed his eyes and tried to calm the pounding in his head. He hadn't had a good meal in days, only nibbling here and there. He couldn't seem to stomach the idea of eating. He knew what was causing it, and it was his fault.

Every day that passed, he lost a little more of himself, and it was only every now and then he could feel like himself. He hadn't been normal in months and, even as he thought that, he felt darkness loom over him. The oily presence slide over his soul. He couldn't remember when that started to happen or when he had stopped fighting it. Had he ever really fought it?

No, because you liked the power.

He closed his eyes and tried his best to fight back the

bile rising in his throat. He spent most of his days fighting the need to throw up...and the headaches. Those left him sick and dizzy, so tired that he couldn't seem to figure out which way was right.

"Sir," his manservant Bellows said.

It took him a few seconds to compose himself. "Yes?"

"There was a late RSVP to the party. The Lennons are coming and they are bringing one extra."

"Phoebe and Callum are coming?" he asked, sick excitement dancing through his blood. He wanted them there at the same time he wanted them to stay away.

He was losing his fucking mind.

"No. They sent their regrets now that Mrs. Lennon is in her last trimester. Instead, Angus, Maggie, and Anice Lennon, along with a Brody Stewart are coming."

Anger filled him as any feelings of remorse faded.

"Was there anything else you needed, sir?"

"No. Thank you."

He said nothing else as he waited for the servant to leave. Once alone, Gavin started to pace. He should have known better than to trust one of the Stewarts. Shifters were...shifty.

He laughed at his joke, the bubble of laughter turned hysterical. Gavin covered his mouth. He should stop this now. It wasn't important. Who gave a flying fuck if the McLennans grabbed the last jewel? If they were stupid enough to give up immortality, then let them.

But it will be your destruction.

The dark voice echoed through the chamber; although, he was sure he was the only one who heard it. It had been happening more and more lately, and he didn't know what to do about it.

He closed his eyes again and tried to block it out, but he knew it wouldn't work. It never did.

You will need your wits about you, Gavin. You need to control the situation.

"But if I doona, I die."

And I will have your soul. If you live, you continue to have wealth and power.

But he didn't have those now. He did when he was handed the job as laird. It was one of the reasons he had thought long and hard about it. He knew that every laird in the last two hundred years had lost their fortunes. And he was dangerously close to doing just that now. He'd sunk his money into finding that bloody amethyst and now, he was throwing a party he couldn't afford just to lure those idiots closer, so he could kill them. Or at least kill Brody. He would take great pleasure in that.

And then, they will continue to suffer.

"Is it that important? Immortality seems like a good thing."

You are a fool. All of your ancestors were, so it makes sense that you are.

Anger and shame lit his temper. When he spoke, he bellowed. "I am not a fool."

Then you do not question this. You do as we order?

"We?"

I mean I. Yes, do as I order.

"I..." He couldn't finish the sentence. Pain speared is head, pulsating out through his entire body. He fell to his hands and knees, breathing in and out, concentrating on pushing the pain away.

Once it had finally subsided, he collapsed on the floor. Gavin drew in a ragged breath.

There was no way of going back.

Chapter Thirteen

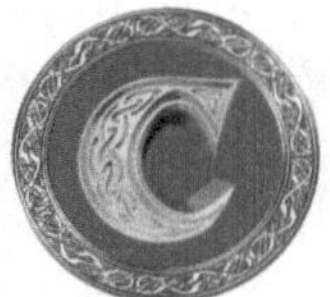

After the family meeting, Brody craved another run, but knew that wasn't going to help. His earlier sprint had taken the edge off his need, but not nearly enough. He seriously doubted that a second run would help. If anything, it would probably make things worse. After being out in the wild wind and enjoying the exercise, he had wanted nothing more than to take the interaction with Anice a step further.

His brother had saved him from making an ass out of himself. One of the many times that had occurred in their long lives.

Being older, Cayden had the expertise of a seasoned wolf, and the years had weighed heavily on him. Their father had been Alpha, but he had relinquished the reigns to his son earlier than most. Their father and mother were sick of the fighting, and Cayden had been chomping at the bit to take on the Alpha role of the Stewarts. It had been disaster…emotionally and physically. They were just now getting their pack in order. Getting their land back was the final step in the process.

And for that, he resisted the allure of Anice. Mostly. That one sniff of her earlier had almost sent him into heat. It was an intoxicating mix of herbal soap and Anice. Her unique womanly scent called to him like no other—human or shifter—had ever before.

His phone buzzed, and he grabbed it. It was his brother Archie sending a picture of himself in the cabin of the private McLennan jet. The caption read, *Unfucking-believable!*

He chuckled. Out of them all, his brother was the dreamer, a bit like Anice in that manner. Brody knew, from what little her family had said, that this was Anice's idea. She had been the driving force behind the quest to break the curse; although, a bit of him wondered why.

Shifters lived long lives. Cats lived the longest, but wolves were right up there in expectancy. Not immortal and maybe that was the difference. He wanted to find her and ask her and was already walking to the door when he stopped himself. To ask a question was a stupid excuse. If he got near her right now, there was a good chance he would lose it and take her to bed. That would not be a good idea.

Why not?

Damn, his wolf was awake and growling.

I'm ready for our mate. I need her near us.

"You're fine," he said out loud.

Not if you're pacing the floor. You know that we need her, we will settle once we have her in bed.

Yet he knew if he got close to her when they were alone, he would seduce her. She would come willingly, but there was a good chance he would lose her in the morning. He could not have that. He needed Anice now and forever.

Start tonight, and worry about tomorrow morning later.

"She would walk away."

Before his wolf could answer, there was a knock on his door. Thinking it was his brother, he opened it. Instead, he found Anice bundled up in a robe, her face scrubbed clean.

She was even more stunning without makeup.

"Do you mind if we chat?"

His wolf practically shuddered with excitement.

"I doona know if that is a good idea, Anice."

"Why not?"

"Because if you come into my room...Why don't we go downstairs?"

She frowned at him. "Anyone could barge in on us, and they usually do around here. I'm sure you've noticed."

"That's true...but," he glanced back at his bed and apparently, she took that as an invitation and stepped over the threshold.

His wolf howled in triumph.

Shut it.

Quit being a coward.

Get bent.

"You're doing it again."

"What?" he asked, giving up and closing the door.

"Talking to your wolf. Or, at least that's what I assume you are doing."

He shook his head.

"You're not?" she asked.

"No. I am, it's just scary how easily you have me figured out."

Something passed over her face that made him wary. And sad. So very sad.

"I wish I did."

"What does that mean?"

"It means I doona know you. Not really."

Brody frowned. "You do. We've been dating a month."

"You've been spying on me."

"I've been falling for you."

She crossed her arms beneath her breasts. "I told you before, you doona have to lie to me anymore."

"I'm not lying to you."

She snorted and looked away, but not before he saw the hope...then the sadness that filled her eyes. It was like a bloody knife to his heart. How had he lost this woman so easily? He had wanted her from the moment he saw her, but as he got to know her, he had come to admire her. He knew her life couldn't have been easy, but she was resilient. She seemed to be the most hopeful out of all of the cousins. She had a unique way of looking at life, and it always amused him to hear her opinion on anything...from world events to the latest rage in reality TV.

He desperately wanted that back. It had only been a day now, but he felt as if he had lost everything. "I'm not. I've been falling for you for weeks now. Months even. From that moment I first saw you."

"Brody, we have things to discuss, so just stop lying."

"Woman, I swear to God...do you know it's taking all of my control not to grab you and strip you naked? You're standing right in front of my bed. I want you on it, under me, moaning my bloody name, and every last shred of my control is holding on by a very thin thread. So doona tell me I'm lying. The truth is, if I didn't care for you, I wouldn't think twice about bedding you. But because I do, because I want a future with you, I'm holding back."

"Oh...well..." her voice trailed off and he realized he might have just overwhelmed her.

"I'm sorry. I didn't mean to talk like that to you."

She continued to stare at him as if he had grown a second head.

Way to sweep her off her feet, wanker.

He didn't say anything else because he would definitely make it worse.

"Okay." She studied him for a second. "You're totally serious?"

He nodded, once.

"Then," she said as she stepped closer. He couldn't help himself. He backed up and found the door at his back.

Coward.

Damn right.

She hesitated again, but then shook her head as if trying to fend off some internal struggle. She crowded him closer, slipping her arms up and over his shoulders. There was that scent again. The herbal soap and more of her. He wanted nothing more than to lose himself in her. His cock throbbed, begging for relief. Bloody hell.

Stop fucking around. She's our mate and she wants us.

"Then I really want you to prove it, Brody."

"What?"

"Take me to bed."

"Again, what?"

She rose up on her toes and pressed her mouth against his. In that quick instant, the entire world dissolved around them. Heat flared as his cock hardened.

Yes.

Her tongue danced over the seam of his lips and he opened them. The taste of her filled his senses as his wolf and he growled in happiness. It only took a couple of seconds and he took over the kiss. He wrapped his arms around her as he slanted his mouth over hers again and again. God, she was delicious, exquisite. He had lost track of the women he'd had over the last few decades, but not one of them would ever be able to compare to Anice.

He reversed their positions, then tore his mouth away from hers. As he sunk to his knees, he tugged at the sash in her robe. It came undone easily and he parted the soft fabric to find that all she wore was a pair of black silky panties.

He glanced up at her. "If I had known this is all you had on beneath your robe, I might have jumped you the moment you walked in the room."

He raised his palm to one breast as he bent his head to take the other nipple into his mouth.

Then he was kissing his way down her body again. He needed a taste of her before he sunk into the glorious warmth. He eased her panties down her legs, tossing them behind him. Without hesitation, he pressed his mouth against her sex. Anice shivered, then groaned in pleasure. The sound of her pleasure sunk into his body, to his wolf...to his soul. He teased her, slipping his tongue between her folds, then up and over her clit.

"Oh, Brody," she moaned as she speared her fingers through is hair. Again and again, he continued the same motion as he added a finger, sliding it deep within her. On the third thrust of his finger, he added another one and she screamed, shuddering against the door as her orgasm took over.

His body wanted this, needed this. Better yet, he was not only going to make himself happy, but also his wolf. Never before had he dealt with a need so powerful. It felt like everything was right in his world as he rose back to his feet, then bent to lift her off the floor into his arms.

He bent his head to kiss her as he walked them over to his bed. He set her on the mattress, then stood back. She was there, naked, and his for the taking.

And in that instant, he knew that he loved her. He waited for the fear, for the denial…neither showed up. Instead, he felt solid, as if he was standing on solid ground for the first time in his life.

His wolf's needs and his own intertwined.

"Brody, is there something wrong?"

He shook his head.

"Are you sure?"

He smiled as he tugged off his shirt, then stepped out of his pants. As he neared the bed, she reached out for him, wrapping her hand around his cock. One stroke and he almost came.

"Whoa, I want to be inside of you before I lose it."

She released him, then nibbled on her bottom lip. "So, I doona get to have you in my mouth?"

Yes. Now please.

"Next time. As I said, you and I together."

She nodded as he joined her on the bed. He wanted more time to play, to touch, to savor…but there was another pressing need.

He did take a moment, though. He rose to his knees and looked down at her. Good God, she was gorgeous. Dark hair, fair skin, those amazing eyes. His gaze dipped down to her breasts. Her nipples were hard, so he couldn't resist reaching out and pinching one, then the other. Her legs moved restlessly on the bed. She arched up, and he dipped his head down to give each nipple a lick. She moaned again, and his wolf howled. Anice was a woman who had no problem showing him her pleasure.

He slipped his hands under her ass and pulled her up. He dipped his head and gave her sex another long lick before lowering her. He had his cock at her entrance and he paused. Again, he looked down at the woman who had entranced him from the moment he had seen her. Her eyes were closed.

"Anice. Look at me." Her lids fluttered, then finally opened. "From now and beyond."

Then, he entered her in one long, hard thrust. They both sucked in a breath. He hadn't breached a maidenhead, but…

"Anice, are you a virgin?"

"Not anymore," she said.

He studied her. "Anice…"

"Doona get mad. I wanted this."

He lowered his forehead to hers as he tried to compose himself. He wanted to lose himself in her, but he knew he had to be careful with her.

He started to move, slowly at first, not wanting to hurt her. Over and over again, he thrust into her, losing a little more of himself every time he did. Anice was right there with him, moving in rhythm with him. As her moans grew louder, he felt his orgasm shifting closer. Finally, he gave into his wolf and allowed him to take control. He lifted himself to his knees, his fingers digging into her flesh as he thrust once….twice…

Her muscles clamped down hard on his cock as she came again. It pulled his cock deeper into her warmth as he gave into his own needs. He poured himself into her.

He collapsed on top of her.

"Bloody hell, you're heavy," she said.

He forced himself to raise up in order to look down at her. Her face was flushed, her eyes were bright with pleasure, and her hair was a tangle of curls over his pillows.

Ours.

He and his wolf said it simultaneously. In that one instant, he knew without a doubt she was going to be his only mate. There could be other women who might have been a better choice, especially since she wasn't too keen on him at the moment. Those women would never call to him like Anice did. She was that one special woman, the one he knew would be a true mate in body and spirit.

"Brody, is something wrong? I'm sorry I didna tell you I was a virgin."

He bent his head and brushed his mouth over hers. "Not a problem, love."

Then he settled on the bed next to her, pulling her close and hoping that one day they would be able to get past his deception and have a life together.

If not, he wasn't sure if he would ever be happy again.

Chapter Fourteen

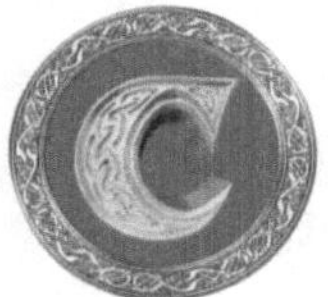

Moments later, Anice was still trying to come to terms with what had transpired. In all her years, she had never felt so complete and at peace with the world. Every now and then, Brody would trail his fingers down her spine. There was a connection, one that she'd felt from the beginning. It went beyond just having things in common or being attracted to him. She had dated men like that before. Never had she wanted to just crawl in the bed and live there. It really had nothing to do with sex. Okay, a bit of it had to do with sex. But she knew there was something different about him…about her when she was with him.

He rose to his elbow and looked down at her. He was so bloody sexy. When he looked at her, she felt…hot. Always. Even when he was confused like right now. And that meant one thing. She was probably in love with him. Nope, not probably. Definitely in love with him, like an idiot.

She waited for the age-old panic. God, she loved him. Not the silly infatuation she thought she had experienced before this. Instead, it was falling head over heels in love with this man. This wolf. Whatever he was. She didn't care. The moment he had thrust into her, she had felt complete, as if everything in her life now made sense. Since she had never had sex before, she wasn't sure if that happened all the time, but she doubted it. The rightness of the feeling had more to do with the connection she felt with Brody rather than with sex. And that was something that worried her more than anything else.

"Why didn't you tell me?" he asked in a quiet, serious tone.

She didn't need to ask what he meant. "I told you. I thought you might rebuke me."

"Are you sure that's all of it?"

He chuckled. "Love, there was absolutely no chance of that happening."

"Do you mean it?"

He nodded, without taking his gaze from her. As they continued to stare at each other, heat flared deep in her belly. Just like that, she wanted him again, wanted to feel him deep within her, claiming her again and again.

"So it doesn't matter if I told you."

"Yes, but I could have been a little more gentle with you."

She smiled. "You were fine."

He raised one hand to his chest and closed his eyes as if in pain. "Dagger to the heart."

"What?"

"Fine is not a word a man wants to hear from a woman he just had the best sex of his life with."

"Brody," she said, "You doona have to lie to me."

"What am I lying about?"

She rolled her eyes. "Really? You had the best sex of

your life with me? The virgin?"

He leaned down and brushed his mouth over hers, all the while keeping his gaze locked with hers. Her heart started beating so hard she was sure he could hear it. "Nothing but the truth, love."

"Brody," she said, even though a tiny part of her heart wanted to believe him. She wanted to think that she had entrapped this amazing, sexy man—with a few bad tendencies, she thought with a silent laugh.

"Anice, I doona lie in bed."

She let one eyebrow rise.

"Okay not with you, though."

She laughed. "Sure," she said as she tried to slip out of bed. He grabbed her arm and pulled her back, tumbling them over the bed so he was on top of her again. His serious expression scared her.

"I'm not lying, love. You blew my mind. Hell, my wolf is exhausted from happiness."

"Brody." But she couldn't continue. He had undone her with what she hoped was his honest tone.

"Listen. I know that you doona have much experience."

"Try none."

"But it isn't always like that."

"Okay."

"Doona bloody placate me."

She sighed. They wouldn't solve anything right now and probably ever. She might have given her body to him, and she might just be losing her heart to him, but she would be bloody insane to accept everything he said at face value.

"Tell me."

"You weren't truthful when we dated. If Gavin hadn't

interrupted us, I would have never known."

"That's not true," he said, in an aggrieved tone. Too bloody bad. He hadn't been truthful with her before. There was no getting around that fact.

"'Tis true and you know it."

"No. There was no way I was walking away from you. I just hadna come up with a way to tell you yet. He just helped it along."

She frowned at him. "Brody, please doona lie to me. I can take a lot, but I canna have you do that to me again."

He leaned down and kissed her, softly at first, then he deepened the kiss, stealing inside of her mouth. She couldn't help but respond. By the time he pulled back, her head was spinning.

"I made a lot of mistakes, but I was going to make it right. I wasna sure quite how, but to hurt you now is to hurt myself, Anice."

"You still lied."

"Okay, I did. I did it for my family. It's dangerous not being on our land and living outside of Scotland wears on us all. The only person in the Clan who doesn't need to be on Scottish land is Eloise. But without the freedom to roam, our lifespan diminishes."

"But your sister is in Texas."

"And she can shift and run there. America has a lot of wolves." He studied her for a long moment, as if trying to figure something out. "Gavin wanted me to bed you right off the bat, but I couldna do it."

"Why not?"

"Because I knew you were my mate. I couldna take you to bed without you knowing who I was truly. He even called me before our date the other night."

"I had other plans when we went out to dinner. Before

Gavin broke it up."

"Well, thank God he did that because I might have proven myself a coward and gave into you. It was a hard fight for me."

She smiled. "Still…"

"You doona have to accept my word now. I will prove myself to you."

She snorted. "I think you already did that."

"I wasn't talking about that. But just so you know, you haven't seen anything yet."

He slipped down her body, teasing her flesh with is mouth. He scraped his teeth over one nipple, then pulled it into his mouth. He gave the same treatment to her other nipple before he kissed his way down her body. With a nip here, and a scrape of teeth there, he had her moaning. She never thought of hiding any of her enjoyment, why would she? And right now, she didn't give a bloody damn about anything but the pleasure he was giving her. When he settled between her legs, he gave her slit one long lick. She shuddered as she felt another wave of liquid heat fill her sex.

He looked up at her and hummed. "You always smell so beautiful, Anice, but right here…it's all you. Sexy, feminine…mine."

She couldn't look way—didn't want to. Even if he hadn't said anything, Anice could read the intent in his eyes. He kept his gaze locked on hers as he bent his head. She felt the graze of his beard first, the light feathery touch teased her even closer to the edge. He slipped his tongue between her folds and she almost came. As she watched his eyes shut, Anice slipped her fingers through his hair, urging him on. She gave herself up to the bliss he offered, the total abandonment to everything but pleasure.

He slipped a finger inside of her while teasing her clit once… twice…with the third graze of his teeth over the tiny bundle of nerves, she came apart, bucking up against his mouth as wave after wave of ecstasy rolled through her.

She was barely recovered from her orgasm when Brody rose from between her legs, flipped her over on her stomach, and then pulled her hips up off the bed. He entered her from behind in one long hard thrust.

They both groaned, the sound echoing throughout the chamber.

He started to move, his fingers digging into her hips, he drove into her again and again.

"Oh, yes," he groaned. "Fuck."

She felt the stirrings of another orgasm start. As she moved in rhythm with him, her body shuddered, the demand for another release growing each time he plunged into her. Then, she tipped over the edge, shouting his name as she came, shuddering as joy took her over.

She thought she was beyond another orgasm, but Brody continued to push her. He had her screaming his name once more before he finally gave into his own pleasure, thrusting into her hard one last time before he poured himself into her.

They collapsed on the bed, but this time he made sure not to smother her. Their heavy breathing was the only sound in the room until she said, "Bloody hell."

He laughed. "Exactly."

They both laughed, until he pulled her back into his arms and covered them with the sheet. She thought she was too revved up to sleep, but she soon felt slumber take hold…then nothing at all.

THE NEXT MORNING, Brody lay in bed watching Anice. He knew it was a little creepy, but he couldn't believe she was actually there, in his bed. He didn't deserve her, he knew that much. He had made love to her three times, but he knew without a doubt, it would never be enough. Until the day he died, he would remember her surrender. He knew there was a good chance that at the end of this quest, they would be over. She would never trust him.

But she could. You have to prove yourself.

He rolled his eyes. I thought you would sleep most of the day.

No. We have work to do. For her. For her family and ours.

She shifted on the mattress and curled closer to him. When they hadn't been making love, they had clung to each other. Brody thought that might be a good sign, but everything was still shaky.

"What are you thinking about?" she asked, her voice groggy with sleep. She didn't open her eyes.

"Just what we have to do. I didna wake you, did I?"

"No." Then it seemed to hit her where she was. Her eyes fluttered open and her cheeks stained red. She was a delight.

"Good morning, love."

"What time is it?" she asked trying to scoot away.

"Not even seven yet," he said, grabbing her and rolling them over the mattress so he was on top of her. He knew they couldn't make love, as she was probably too sore, but it didn't stop his cock from having a mind of its own.

"Brody."

"Anice, don't."

"Don't what?"

"Be ashamed."

Her eyes widened. "Why would I be ashamed?"

"You're not?"

She shook her head. "It's, well you know you were my first and I have no idea what to do."

He frowned. "What are you supposed to be doing?"

"Exactly. What do people do the morning after?"

Then it hit him. She had never had to deal with this, or the fact that her family was definitely going to know. He didn't give a bloody damn, but her family was important to her.

"Do whatever you feel like doing."

"I...I doona know what I want to do." Then she shifted and winced. He knew that he had put her in pain with their escapades the night before.

"Why don't we take a shower?"

"Just a shower?"

"Sure."

No.

He rolled off her, then up to his feet. He bent down to slip his arms beneath her legs and back, lifting her off the mattress.

"Brody," she said. "You're going to hurt yourself."

"No. You're light as a feather."

"We both know *that* is a lie."

"No. You are light to me, but I am a wolf. I have more strength."

A bubble of laughter rose up. "I think you just disparaged me."

He stopped walking. "There is nothing I would do to hurt you. You have to understand that whatever I do to you, will hurt me."

She nibbled on her bottom lip. "Is that a mate thing?"

He nodded, then his gaze dropped down to her breasts.

Yes.

No. She needs a break.

"Brody," she said, her voice embarrassed again.

"What? I've seen you naked, love."

And tasted every bit of her flesh.

"At night."

"The lights were on. So doona be ashamed."

"I'm not. It's just…I'm not used to this."

He nodded and set her down on her feet in the bathroom. He started the shower, then stepped back for her to step in before him.

He followed her, enjoying the heated water against his flesh. She wasn't the only one who'd had a workout the night before.

But she wasn't able to get any water with him standing in front of it. He reversed their positions and almost groaned as the water slipped down her body, leaving her curves slick. He couldn't resist leaning forward to lick a drop of water as it dangled off her nipple.

"I thought we were just going to have a shower," she said, a husky edge to her voice.

Forget that, you wanker. She wants us.

"Yes. Turn, so I can wash your back."

She studied him for a second, then did as he asked. He grabbed the soap and that was a mistake. It was the same one that she used. The herbal scent filled the shower. *Bloody hell.*

He pushed those thoughts aside and lathered up the soap. He touched his hands to her back, washing and massaging it at the same time. She set her hands on the wall in front of her, then hung her head down. The long moan wasn't sexual at all. Instead, it was a release of tension and probably a little pain. He worked his hands down her back, pressing his thumbs hard against her spine, just enough to help release some of the tension he found there. She shuddered and moaned again--this time it was definitely sexual.

She turned around and faced him. In that moment, he didn't know what to say or do. He could blame it on the blood loss to his brain, but he knew better. He knew that it had more to do with him being lost in this woman. His mate. He wanted her with such power that it was embarrassing, but he didn't know how to handle that. He felt out of his element, unable to say anything.

"Brody?" she asked. He shook his head.

"Are you okay?"

He nodded.

Then she smiled, and he felt as if he owned the whole bloody world. "Good, because I have one or two things I would like to do to you."

"I think maybe you should take it easy."

Shut it.

She wrapped her hand around his cock and gave him a long stroke, her fingers dancing over the tip. If he didn't know better, he would have never known she'd lost her virginity just a few short hours ago.

Her thumb grazed the head again, this time capturing a bit of his precum. She raised it to her mouth looking up at him as she did, and licked it off her finger.

"Hmm," she said.

Bloody hell. Need her now.

Before he could act on his wolf's demand, she dropped to her knees and took him into her mouth. As she licked and sucked his cock, she slid her fingers over his sac. With each swipe of her tongue, he danced closer to that edge. He molded his hands to the back of her head as she continued teasing him with her mouth. Soon, though, he knew he was getting too close to pull back. He wanted her with him when he came.

"Enough," he said grabbing her to pull her up.

She frowned, but he didn't have the patience to tell her exactly why he stopped her. Instead, he lifted her up, bracing her back against the tiled wall. He positioned his cock at her entrance and slowly entered her. His body was begging for him to go fast, fast, fast. Hell, his wolf was growling at him, but he knew she was a bit tender from the night before. Her muscles clung to him each time he pulled out then drove back into her. Soon though, the easy rocking motions weren't enough to satisfy him. He increased his rhythm, plunging deeper and deeper inside of her with each thrust. It only took a few thrusts and she was coming, pulling him along for the ride.

He held her tight after his orgasm, knowing that this moment would not last.

"Brody?"

He pulled back and looked down at her as he eased out of her.

"Come on," he said urging her under the water.

He soaped her up again, taking pleasure in the quiet moment, the almost serene atmosphere now. Together, they cleaned up, and even though he knew they needed to get downstairs, he took her back to his bed. He pulled her into his arms, holding her tightly against his heart. For now, this was going to have to be enough.

Chapter Fifteen

By the time they made it down to breakfast, most the family was already at the table. The only time that happened was when she was sick. Still, she refused to feel guilty.

Well, not *that* guilty.

After their shower together, she had hurried back to her room. She could care less if she ran into her brother or one of her cousins. She didn't, however, want to run into Jack and have to explain what was going on. It was silly, but she felt as if she needed to set an example for him. Truth was that he probably knew all the idiotic stuff about mates that Brody had been spouting off.

She urged Brody to go as soon as he was dressed. He smiled and said nothing, but she was relieved when she entered the dining room and found him sitting at the table drinking coffee. Relief filtered through her. Again, she didn't give a bloody damn about what her cousins or brother thought, but she needed coffee to deal with them. And food. She was ravenous.

She filled her plate and grabbed a coffee before slipping into the chair across from her brother and beside Brody. Sitting this close to him, she felt another wave of relief filter through her. What the hell was that about? She needed to stop listening to him spout off about being her mate. While she had hoped for more at the beginning of their relationship, she now knew it would be impossible. It didn't mean she couldn't enjoy the connection though.

"About time you made it down," her brother grumbled.

Rena groaned. "Fletcher, leave it."

He opened his mouth, but her soon to be sister-in-law shook her head. Unbelievably, he listened to her. Anice was liking having another sibling through marriage. *IF* she could keep Fletcher from making an ass out of himself, she might just not have to kill her twin.

Still, he kept shooting daggers at Brody, who ignored him. He was eating as much as she was and paying attention only to her. He didn't say anything, but he kept giving her looks.

"So, I think it unfair that the M and M's were allowed to see Brody as a wolf and the rest of us missed out," Rena announced.

"I saw him," Anice said.

"I just bet you did," Rena said with a chuckle.

Anice's face heated and she ducked her head and kept eating.

"I saw him too," Jack said. "He promised he wouldn't eat me."

"I would think not. We doona eat little boys," Cayden said, a smile playing about his lips.

"That's just what Brody said, but since I have never met a wolf before, I had to be sure."

"Very wise, in my humble opinion," Cayden said.

"Yes," Jack said.

Anice snorted. The boy definitely didn't have a problem with confidence these days.

"We have a problem," Maggie said, stomping into the room.

"What?" Anice asked.

"The amethyst isn't at his house."

"What? I thought you said he bought it."

"He did. In fact, he didn't even try to conceal it. Instead, he's been flaunting it, but the spy I have in his employ—"

"He's my spy, my lady," Belvidore said.

"Yes. Your spy. Either way, the amethyst had been kept in a secure room until yesterday."

"Did they give a reason for the move?" Anice asked.

"They said it was because of the party he's throwing tonight. He's been telling everyone he took it to the bank and put it in a safety deposit box. I call bollocks."

"Mommy. You said that wasn't a good thing to say," Jack said.

"Sorry, my sweet boy," she said, walking over to him. "It's kind of a bad thing, and this is a bad situation."

"We'll figure it out," Brody said.

"Knowing Phoebe, she's already found something that tells us everything," Anice said. "She was just saying that passages about the quests appear or are easier to translate when their time comes."

"Like my ancestors set it up that way? I doona doubt it. She's right. They are a bunch of barmy witches," Maggie said, sitting down next to her son.

Callum stepped into the room and came up short. "Was there a family meeting called?"

"No. And I have no idea where Meghan and Logan are," Fletcher said.

"Or Angus. Where is he?"

"He went into the office today. He thought it was important to get some things done before we started planning for the party."

"It's odd that he's having the party on Sunday, doona you think?"

"There has to be some kind of significance."

"There is," Phoebe said from the doorway. She was still wearing her robe, and her hair was all over the place.

"Love, you said you would rest," Callum said, rushing to her side. "You didn't sleep well last night."

"No. I didn't. I kept having strange dreams. Odd ones that seemed to make no sense. There was a lot of wind, and it was up in the highlands."

He led her to her chair. "Do you want some tea?"

Belvidore was there with the teapot and a cup before Callum could get an answer the question.

"So, this dream..." Anice asked, feeling a little guilty. Phoebe wasn't doing well, she knew that. Her skin was pale and there were dark circles under her eyes. She knew that it was important that they do something to end this quest.

"You need to eat."

Again, Belvidore appeared. This time with a bowl full of oatmeal that she knew Phoebe loved and some fruit.

"Oh, thank you, Belvidore."

"Of course, my lady."

"You didn't get *me* anything," Callum commented.

"You're not carrying the heir," Belvidore said as he walked out the door.

Anice giggled.

"One word, and I will have you thrown out of the Clan."

"Get over yourself," Phoebe said with a smile. "Get something to eat while I talk about the dream and the passage I just revealed."

He said nothing else and did as she ordered.

"Now. The dream. I was walking in this area. It reminded me of Balmoral."

"You've been there?" Cayden asked.

"Yes. My first husband was related to the royal family. Very distantly. Anyway, it was definitely the highlands, but it wasn't Balmoral. It was surrounded by some forests and then there was a pond not too far from this massive keep. Almost like a castle, but not really."

Anice's skin prickled. Her brother looked over at her.

"What?" Phoebe asked.

"What else did you see, love?" Callum asked as he sat down next to her.

"I saw this path that went into the dark forest, I was scared to go, but also I wanted to go. I could smell heather in the air. As I walked along the path, I came to a house. A little cottage with smoke coming out of the chimney and a cute herb garden out front."

"Bloody hell," Callum muttered.

"What?"

When no one said anything, Anice answered. "You just described the witch's cottage and our old keep. It always smelled like heather."

"Well. That's kind of weird."

"What happened when you went to the cottage?" she asked.

"I walked closer and I could hear the witch...I just assumed it was a normal woman in my dream...but I could hear her saying that day of the year is always important. Just as I got close enough to peek inside, I woke up. Irritated me to no end."

"Eat," Callum ordered.

"Oh, yeah," she said picking up the spoon and nibbling on her oats. "I got up and found my diary open on my beside table. I *know* it was closed when I went to sleep last night. Oh no! I left it upstairs."

"I have it here, my lady."

Callum frowned again, and there were a few more giggles around the table. Callum tossed an aggravated look at them all, which just made them laugh even more.

"So, here is the passage it was opened up to. 'The protector with two souls and the *Key* will find the final jewel amongst the memories of the past. There, in the shadows, they will discover the jewel. But heed the warning, if you do not truly believe, in fate and destiny, then you will lose everything. Past transgressions have no place in this new era'."

There was a long silence after she spoke the words.

"Do you know what that means?" Phoebe asked.

"I kind of understand it," Anice said when no one else answered.

"So, problem solved." She set the diary down and started eating her breakfast in earnest. The entire table stared at her.

"Love?"

"Yes?" she said between bites.

"We doona completely understand."

She had the spoon in her mouth, as she looked up around the table. She finished swallowing her oats. "Oh, sorry. I was just so hungry."

"That seems to be going around this morning," Fletcher said, tossing a look in Anice's direction.

"Drop it," she said.

"Is there a problem?" Callum asked.

Fletcher opened his mouth to answer, but Rena saved them all from a horrible fight.

"No. Fletcher needs to grow up. Phoebe?"

She looked between Fletcher and Anice, then looked at Brody. "Hmm, okay. My interpretation, since you said that it was your home, is that the amethyst is back at the witch's cottage. I know it doesn't make sense, as I know it doesn't make sense since the amethyst is here according to Maggie."

"But it isn't here," Maggie said.

"What?" Callum asked.

"I found out this morning that it was moved for security reasons," she said using air quotes when she said the word security.

"Do you think that maybe there's a reason for this?" Callum asked.

"Sure. He wants us to try and steal the jewel and then he can have us arrested."

"But do we know where it is? I mean, we know that it is somewhere on your land. But the cottage is probably gone, so we would have to figure that out."

"I just know that both you and Anice need to be on your way today. It is that urgent."

"What about the party?"

"There has to be some reason he wants to have the party on a Sunday night."

"It's a full moon," Esme said from the doorway. Anice didna know how long she had been standing there. "Power, good and bad, are at their height that night. Full moons are an amazing night. Plus, this one will be considered a harvest moon. Closer than the rest of the year, and bigger and brighter."

"There's another thing we have to consider. He wants to split us up. The more places we have to cover, then the harder it will be to fight what comes after us," Maggie commented.

"I have to agree with that. He's a slimy bastard. One who should—"

"Doona say it."

Esme continued as if he hadn't said anything. "Have his bits and pieces cut off."

"I said doona say it."

She shrugged and walked over to get herself some coffee.

"Brody and I need to go to our land," Anice said.

"You still own it?"

She nodded. "We doona live there because..."

"You can't?"

"Not in a physical way. It's hard on all of us to be there."

"But you will do it."

"Anything. We will have to get packing."

"I think I should go with you," Esme said.

"What?"

"You need a magickal person with you. At least one. I should go."

"I agree," Maggie said. "With Archie here, we should be good in that department."

"Archie's here?" Brody asked.

"He's out for a run," Cayden said.

"Well, that's rude. He didna even come get me."

"No. He did. He said that you didna answer your door," Cayden said.

Brody's cheeks turned ruddy.

"I thought I heard my name," a man said from the doorway. There was no doubting this was one of the Stewart brothers. He had the same shade of dark hair, same blue eyes, but there was a mischievous air about him. There was no Clan business weighing heavy on him as with Cayden.

"Archie," Brody said, rising from his chair. As soon as he did, Esme took it.

"They haven't seen each other in a few months," she said.

Anice nodded.

"Are you okay?" Esme asked.

"Yes. Why do you ask?"

"No reason. Here, take his bacon. He doesn't really need it."

"Why?"

"Because it will irritate him and that's my job."

Anice laughed as Esme took a couple pieces for herself, then dumped the remaining three on Anice's plate.

"Get out of my seat, you degenerate witch."

She stood. "Remember. I'm going to be protecting you."

Then she flounced off. He looked down at his plate. "Dammit, she stole my bacon again. Have you eaten, Archie?"

"Yes, but I could eat more. Runs make me hungry, but you know that. You must be Anice," he said, taking her hand and raising it to his lips. "So wonderful to meet the woman who put my brother in his place."

"Hands off." Brody growled.

Archie leaned closer and winked at her. "I'm the best looking as man and wolf. You should know that."

"Sod off," Brody said, pushing his brother away.

"Fine way to treat the baby of the family," he said.

"You aren't the baby."

"The baby boy, then."

"Boys…the right term."

"Enough," Cayden said. "Bloody hell, you two give me a headache."

Archie grabbed what Anice was sure was his second plate. "So, what's going on? Cayden explained some of it, but I have a feeling there is more to it than I've heard."

"Gavin moved the stone."

"I always hated that wanker," Archie said.

"As a result, we need to go up there and get the jewel."

"I'm assuming it's up there on your land," Phoebe said.

"Your instincts are never wrong, love," Callum said. "And while it might not be at the witch's cottage, that might have been shown to establish that it is on our land."

She nodded.

"I guess we'll need to start on our way. If Gavin has already moved it, then he's staying here, thinking that we will be distracted," Brody said.

Why was panic rolling through her blood all of the sudden? Was it because she knew that the end was near or that once they got the jewel, she would walk away from Brody? That was what she was planning, right? Just a fling. A little fun.

"Wait. Does anyone think we are rushing this?" Anice asked.

"It seems that way," Phoebe said. "But I will do a little

more reading and thinking, even after you leave. You know I often find things out after we know where the jewel is."

"Meanwhile, we'll keep an eye on Gavin," Maggie said. "And we will go to his stupid thing tonight. We won't rescind your RSVP until you get up country, just in case," she said to Anice. "Better that he thinks he fooled us."

Anice nodded. "I guess I better pack my warmest clothes, she said with a laugh.

"Wait? Where are your lands?" Esme asked.

"Up near Ratagan," Brody answered. Anice looked at him. So many people had no idea that their lands were up in the Scottish Highlands. He shrugged. "I researched."

"What now? You mean up there?" Esme asked pointing to the ceiling. "It's cold up there."

"You're Scottish," Cayden said, disdain dripping from every word.

"It's cold. Like, really bloody cold."

Brody winked at Anice. "I'm sure a better witch would be able to come up with some kind of spell to keep herself warm."

That earned him a slap to the back of the head. "You know I can."

"Since I am not a witch, I will get to packing. I guess we can take one of the SUVs?" she asked Callum, who nodded. "Nice to meet you, Archie."

She picked up her mug and went to gather up her plate—they didn't expect to be waited on—but Brody grabbed it and stacked it on his plate.

"I can get that."

"Yes, but you have more planning to do."

"Is that because I'm a woman?"

"No. It's because I know you need to plan the trip,

plan your packing, and then start packing—even though I know we probably won't stay overnight."

He gave her a cocky smile, then carried the plates out of the dining room. The entire room had gone silent. She glanced around.

"What?"

"I hate to say it, but that wolf sure knows you," Angus said with a chuckle.

"Oh, sod off," she said and stomped out of the room. It didn't matter how well he knew her, he would never truly understand her heart. For that, she needed someone who could be honest with her, and that was something Brody had failed at several times already.

If there was one thing that could be said about Anice McLennan, it was that she didn't suffer liars.

Chapter Sixteen

They were two hours into their trip when Brody decided that something was definitely off. Anice was barely speaking to him and Esme was deep in thought. He didn't need too much conversation, but both women seemed to be somewhere else. "How much do you remember about your land?" Brody asked.

She shrugged. "A little. My favorite part was the fields."

"The fields?"

He glanced over and saw the small smile curving her lips.

"What?"

"I would steal out at night. Not that often, and I would always remain on our land."

"So rebellious."

She laughed. "My brother and cousins were always running around, more than likely sniffing around women, but I had to stay close to home. The lone female stuck in the keep. So, to get away, I would wait for everyone to go to bed, then I would sneak out. I loved the freedom the night gave me."

"Why particularly the night?" Esme asked from the backseat.

"I'm not sure. I was always drawn outside at night. I loved the scents, the animals, and the stars. Especially during a full moon."

"Hmm," Esme said.

Anice turned to look at her. "Do you think that is significant?"

"Maybe. I mean, you are involved with a family of wolves now. And while we doona shift simply because there is a full moon, it does call to us. Both sides of the family."

"Well..."

She said nothing for a moment or two, as if lost in thought or a memory.

"What?" he asked, wanting to know everything about her. He was greedy for any tidbit about her.

"There was one night that the witch found me in a field. She was clearly interested in my nocturnal habits."

"Another link," Esme said.

"I bet if I sat down with my cousins, we could come up with a 500-page book listing all the weird happenings that turned out to have something to do with the curse."

"So, you didn't stay in Scotland, from what I gather. Where did you go?" Esme asked. He glanced at his cousin in the rearview mirror and saw her understanding smile. She knew he wanted to know more about Anice, but if he prodded her, there was a good chance she would shut down.

"We went to the continent. I wanted to go to America, but the stupid boys I live with decided that would be a bad idea. So, we were in Europe for a hundred years or so." She chuckled. "I never say things like that out loud."

"I can't imagine what it was like to live with a bunch of boys like that. No other women around."

"It wasn't easy. They were always a little overprotective."

"They just wanted to make sure you were safe."

"I can take care of myself."

"Back then, it was different."

"Remind me to smack you when we stop to eat. By the way, are we going to do that soon?" Esme asked.

"I think we can grab a bite to eat in the next town," Anice said. "Better we doona eat in the area around our land."

"Why?" Esme asked.

"We would be conspicuous," he said. Three strangers show up, one having a remarkable resemblance to the former young lady who once roamed the lands at night, and we'll draw attention to us."

"As it is, we will be there after dark anyhow, but I think it best to make sure to get there with as little notice as possible."

<hr>

MAGGIE FELT the shift of air the moment they stepped into the McWalton home. Mansion was more like it, but not the wonderful house she lived in now. No, this was decadent. Gold was splashed everywhere, the best of everything. And, as she noted, the air. It was almost as if there was an illness in the air. Like a sickroom that needed to be aired out. Normal folks would merely feel it but not understand it. She knew what it meant though.

Evil lived here.

"Are you all right, love?" Angus asked.

She turned toward her husband and smiled. She hated dressing up. The heels were starting to get to her already, and she wanted tonight to be over. Still, she loved seeing the most handsome man in the world in a tux. She couldn't wait until this was all over and she could get him in that kilt. He was so damned sexy in it, but they didn't wear the McLennan plaid outside of family gatherings and weddings.

"Just...something's not right here."

He nodded. "I feel it."

They walked around the room and chatted with people they knew. Since she had gotten involved with the McLennans, she had become more adept at handling these situations, but still, there was an icy finger tracing her spine. Was it the dark magick Gavin had been playing with, or was it something even worse? Was there anything worse?

There was the tinkling of a bell.

"Please join us in the dining room for light refreshments," Bellows said.

They discovered that they had seating requirements. When they sat, the places for Anice and Brody were empty, of course.

A well-dressed gentleman appeared, wearing a tux and looking a little uncomfortable.

"Thank you all for coming to the fundraiser. I and Mr. McWalton believe in Scotland's independence. We need another referendum on the issue and soon."

He raised a glass. "To Scotland."

Everyone raised their glasses, but Maggie caught her

husband's eye and shook her head. He gave her a questioning look.

She leaned in close to whisper, "We have no idea if there is anything in the drinks. Better safe than sorry."

He nodded and put down his glass.

"Now, enjoy the light dinner, along with an amazing dessert." He stepped away and walked in their direction. Angus caught his attention, so the man stopped.

"Hello, Gerald. This is my wife Maggie."

He nodded in her direction and smiled. This wasn't a McWalton. More like an errand boy, but Angus knew him, so he must have met him in business.

"Nice to meet you."

"I thought Gavin was going to be here?" Angus asked.

Now, the nerves were back. He glanced from side to side, as if to make sure no one was watching or listening. "Gavin was called away on an urgent business matter."

"Oh?"

"Yes."

"But you doona know what it might be?"

Gerald shook his head. "It had something to do with the personal side of the business. You know what those big Clans are like."

He nodded. "Of course. We are looking forward to the auction. I'll let you go, as I know there are a number of people wanting to talk to you."

He nodded. "Again, nice to meet you, Mrs. Lennon."

Then he was gone.

"That's weird."

"No, it's not. I have a bad feeling about this," Maggie said, pulling out her phone. "You think he went up there, don't you?" he whispered, then kissed her temple. Anyone watching them would think they were just a loving couple.

"I need to text both Anice and Phoebe."

He nodded. "Steal away and I will follow."

She gave him a kiss, then rose out of her chair, taking her purse with her. She knew he would come behind her and have her back. That little thought filled her with warmth, even as she felt another tremor of cold seep into her blood. Something was definitely wrong.

She pulled out her phone and started to text Phoebe and Anice.

Gavin isn't here.

Phoebe: What? He didn't show up to his own fundraiser?

Nope.

Anice: What do you think it means?

I worry he knows where you are headed, and we sent you into a trap. I still say that we should have figured out a way to get all three of you up to the property with magick.

It could be done, but even with several magickal folks, it could have left them too weak for any kind of battle.

She felt Angus step up behind her.

"Any word?"

She shook her head.

Anice: Too much of a risk.

Phoebe: True, but since he isn't there, come back to the house. Callum and Rena agree. No reason to risk it.

On our way now.

"We're leaving," she said and started to walk toward the exit. A blast of cold air hit them, and she fell back into Angus.

"What the bloody hell was that?"

"Could be a ward."

"Those are to keep people out, right?"

"Or to trap them, but bugger that."

She chanted a spell to break it and, thankfully, it crumbled. A rush of warmth surrounded them. "Let's get out of here before the bastard realizes we broke through."

Angus nodded, took her hand, and hurried out of the house. As they started off to the car, a clap of thunder sounded. The ground beneath them shook, and all of the outside lights that surrounded the mansion flashed...then blinked out.

"What the bloody hell was that?" Angus asked. The wind started to whirl around them. "Forget that. What the hell is this?"

"Get the car," she said, as she closed her eyes to chant.

"If you think I'm going to leave you right now, you're daft."

She opened her eyes and cupped his face. After a long moment of staring into his eyes, she said, "I canna concentrate with you here. I'm going to fight this off while you get the car. Then we can get the hell out of here."

"What about transporting?"

She shook her head. "It will only drain me, and I know this is just a prelude."

He nodded and gave her a hard, quick kiss, then ran toward their car. She closed her eyes again and started chanting. Power surged within her as she raised her hands. Evil snapped in the air around her. She knew it wasn't an entity. She could feel that it had been a trap of sorts, one that would keep them from leaving, still, not a particularly big threat. It didn't mean that it could be ignored. There was definitely a darkness in it, one that she knew could fester and end up hurting others. Chanting, she lashed out at it, sparks flying in the air around her as a wall of darkness grew in intensity.

Heat flew out at her. Maggie stumbled back but

regained her footing with no problem. Even as fear chilled her blood, she stood her ground. Gritting her teeth, she fought back with her white magick, all the while, ignoring the small cuts in her flesh and Angus yelling at her.

With one last chant to dispel the evil, she pushed back against the dark force. There was another large clap of thunder, one that shook the ground...then, the wind stopped and the energy around the mansion seemed to calm.

Angus ran up to her. "What the bloody hell do you think you were doing?"

Suddenly she was slammed up against his chest and he wrapped his arms around her. It was only at that point that she let the fear and panic take over. Tears burned her eyes, as she wrapped her arms around Angus.

She pulled back and looked up at him. "Doona cry, love," he said brushing away her tears.

She nodded. "Thank you."

"For what."

She didn't really know how to express the love she felt for him, how he had given a family to her and Jack, and for always being right by her side for every fight.

"For being you."

He gave her another kiss, just like the one earlier. "Let's get the hell out of here. I've had enough of this crap."

She laughed and nodded. They were on their way home when her phone buzzed.

Anice: Are you free?

Yes. Should be back at the house in less than half an hour. Be careful. He thought this through.

Phoebe: Be safe and get home quickly.

Maggie turned around and watched as the McWalton

mansion grew smaller and smaller. For the first time in hours, she felt a little more at ease.

"I hated being there."

He nodded. "I'll feel better when we're at the house."

She settled back in her seat and sent good thoughts to Anice, Brody, and Esme.

THEY HAD JUST ARRIVED on McLennan land when their car died. Anice's senses went into hyper alert as the hair on her arms stood up. Bloody hell, that definitely wasn't good.

"Well, that's not a promising sign," she said.

"No. And I have a really bad feeling right now," Esme said. "There's some extremely bad magick in these parts."

"Do we need to worry about the owners? I can't believe I didn't ask about that before we left."

She shook her head. "We *are* the owners. Callum bought all the land back a while ago."

"So, I'm in charge," Esme said.

"What?" Brody asked.

"I'm the one who will sense the magick. You need to listen to me."

They sat in silence for a few seconds. Her mobile ringing jarred all of them and pulled a laugh from her.

"It's Phoebe," she said clicking the speaker on. "What's up? You're on speaker by the way."

"Angus and Maggie made it back home safely."

"Good," Anice said.

"How goes it there?"

"The car died the moment we hit our land."

"Well, that's a bad sign."

"I said pretty much the same. Do you have anything else we need to know?"

"Yes. I translated another passage. *The Key and her protector are the most powerful of all of them. Together, they can conquer anything. Sacrifice is not truly the end, but the beginning.*"

"That's it?" Brody asked. "Our family is annoying."

Normally Phoebe would laugh, but she did not. That was how tense things were at the moment.

"Anything for me, Phoebe?" Esme asked.

"No. I feel that you are in the blasted diary, but it isn't letting me see it yet."

"Yep. I'm with you, Brody. Our family is definitely annoying."

"Let's get going," Anice said. "The longer we chat, the later it is getting."

"Yes. Of course. Be safe and make sure to let us know what happened; although, we will probably know before you call."

"Be safe, yourself."

She clicked off the phone.

"What does she mean? They will probably know?" Brody asked.

"When we retrieve a stone, it disappears and then reappears in the sword."

"So bloody cool," Esme said. "Now I kind of wished I stayed there."

"Same plan though, we know for sure that bastard is up here," Brody said.

Anice drew in a deep breath, then released it slowly. "Let's do this."

"Anice," Brody said.

"I'll wait outside," Esme said, slipped from the SUV to give them privacy.

"I wanted to say that we will have a long talk when this is all over."

She shook her head. "There's no reason, Brody."

"Yes. There is."

"It doesn't matter." When he opened his mouth to argue with her, she stopped him. "It doesn't. Not now. All I care about is getting that amethyst. You owe me nothing."

His eyes turned darker. He was definitely not happy about the situation, but he nodded. She was in charge of her life from now on and she wasn't going to have a man dictate to her what needed to be said, how they needed to go along. She had had enough of that. Now all that mattered was breaking this bloody curse.

"All right," he said. "Let's go find this bloody amethyst."

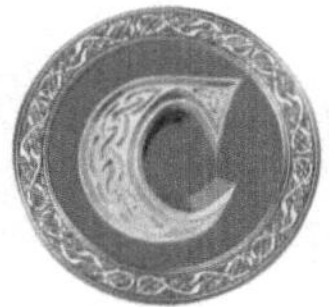

Chapter Seventeen

Irritation slinked down Brody's spine, but he ignored it. Mostly. He couldn't really. They had bad things to conquer and a curse to break. And besides, he kind of deserved the rebuke. He had lied to her about who he was and then again about what he was. Just because she gave him her virginity didn't really mean anything. Not in this day and age.

She is not from this time.

Oh, shut it. I need my wits about me.

You need to shift.

He ignored his wolf as much as he could. He was always there, right below the surface. Currently, though, his wolf was ready for a fight. The air snapped with danger. He knew he was more lethal as a wolf, but until he needed to fight, he wanted to stay on two legs.

Anice's mobile buzzed again.

"A message from Phoebe. The last treasure can be found where the *Key* found solace."

She blinked and looked up at him.

"Do you know what that means?" Brody asked.

"I...does it mean now or back then?"

"I would say back then," Esme said. "This all pertains to who you were before the curse, so it would be back then. Was there a favorite place you always ended up? A place you went to when you felt you needed to either hide or have some freedom."

Her face lit up and she smiled, then it dissolved. "I used to wander the fields at night. Remember?"

It was the story that she had told them on the way up there. He nodded. "Where in the fields?"

"The bloody fields," she said, her voice cracking. "How will we figure that out?"

Esme stepped forward and took her free hand, urging Anice to look at her. "I need you calm. Take a deep breath. Think. Is there a specific memory, one that you can pinpoint might have been a sign?"

Anice sighed and closed her eyes. "It was so long ago."

Esme gave Brody a look, then gestured with her head for him to take Anice's hand. Anice opened her eyes briefly.

"Give me your mobile or put it in your pocket. Hold onto Brody with two hands."

Anice did as she ordered and closed her eyes again. As soon as she did, Brody felt a jolt of energy rush through his system. He'd had that feeling before when he was with her, but it hadn't been this intense. She shook, and he held on tighter.

"Concentrate, Anice. One moment, one little thing that might have not seemed like a big thing, but you know now that it was."

Another jolt, heat spreading out through his body as he felt her shake even more. In the next instant, she opened her eyes.

"I remember. It was the night of the full moon when your ancestor found me. There is a wishing well nearby. Come on."

She released his hands and turned to run away, but he grabbed her.

"Be careful, love. We doona know where Gavin is."

She sighed and nodded. "It's just up this path," she said, pointing to a dirt trail that wound through a bunch of trees.

He nodded and stepped in front of her. "Me in front and Esme behind you. All of us need to keep our wits about us."

He started on his way, certain she was right. Even as he thought that, he knew without a doubt there was something very, very wrong. Each step took them closer to their destiny, but he knew without a doubt, Gavin was somewhere in the area. Even if Maggie hadn't told them, he would know. That darkness seemed to permeate the entire forest.

Careful. We need to keep both her and you safe.

I know.

The wind shifted, and the stench of sulfur surrounded them.

"I should have known that he would be playing with a demon," Esme muttered.

"What?" Anice asked.

"That smell. It's a sign of demons and anyone associated with the devil. Gavin is such a lazy ass bastard. I want him to cry when we are done with him."

"Esme," he warned.

"I know. I should keep focused, and I am, it's just that he denies us our rights, and his ancestors killed their own blood because of their abilities. Then he bastardizes it by playing with demons."

A tree branch cracked above them. Fear and panic filled him as he turned to grab Anice to save her. Thankfully, she was already moving toward him, and Esme had followed her. The branch hit the ground with a thud.

Bastard.

"Bastard," Esme muttered at the same time.

"Let's hurry. I know we need to be safe, but the sooner we are there, the faster we can see if I am right."

As they stepped out of the forest, a large field was there. The scent of heather fought with another odor that made his eyes water. Sulphur again.

"This is it," Anice said, her hushed reverence spoke to him. This was indeed the place. He didn't doubt it. The rightness of it sunk into his bones and his wolf actually hummed.

Brody pulled out the dagger he had brought with him. Until he had to shift, he wanted some kind of protection. As soon as they stepped into the field, a flash of lightening then thunder cracked above them. A rush of cold air hit them so hard they stumbled.

"Take her," Esme said.

"Esme—"

"No, go. I will push back on him, so you have some time."

He nodded and grabbed Anice's hand and hurried through the field. It was overgrown, making it so difficult.

"Esme," Anice shouted.

"She will take care of him for us."

She stopped, and he had to tug on her hand. When he glanced back, he realized there was large dark cloud, at least twenty stories high in front of his cousin. The wind blew her hair around and she was moving around, power sparking off her hands as she fought Gavin and whatever black magick he had conjured.

"Come on. She'll be fine," he said, tugging on her hand. At the same time, he sent a prayer to his cousin, hoping that his faith in her would hold true.

As they ran through the fields, the air grew heavier. It was hard to gain a good breath, but they kept on. The sounds of the fight behind them tore at his heart. He didn't know what his cousin was going through.

They continued on until a horrible sound exploded behind them. It lanced through his soul. He almost doubled over from the pain, but he gritted his teeth and kept on. He wanted to protect his cousin, but he knew she was part of this fight. He had to let her do what was needed as he protected Anice.

"There it is!" Anice exclaimed.

He followed her direction and saw the well at the end of the field. They rushed forward and just as they were about fifty yards from it, something shifted in the air. Intense dread filled the atmosphere.

They reached the wishing well and found the bucket down. He took hold of the handle and started to retrieve it as Anice looked around the area.

"What are you doing?" he asked as he continued on his task.

"I just wanted to make sure it wasn't anywhere else."

She turned and came toward him as the bucket rose out of the well. He grabbed it. There, in the bottom of the worn wood, was a perfect amethyst.

"Well," she said stepping closer as he reached in and grabbed the jewel.

Instantly, an energy seemed to explode around them.

Dirt, rocks, and grass flew everywhere. He covered Anice, trying to protect her from the worst of it, all the while, he held onto the jewel. When everything settled, he stood. Gavin stood in front of them, but not the man Brody had known most of his life. Brody would bet that very little of Gavin remained.

Let me at him.

He agreed with is wolf, but the insane woman he was in love with, stepped in front of him. Brody tried to pull her back and she shook her head. "I'm immortal."

"It doesn't mean that he can't make you hurt."

The laughter that filled the air sent a chill down his spine and brought out a snarl from his wolf.

"Do you actually think you can beat me? Your cousin is more powerful than you are, and I vanquished her."

"If you hurt Esme, I will end you," Anice shouted. Brody looked at her as he moved to stand beside her. This was his mate. She had her hands fisted on her hips as she dared to confront a man who was playing with dark magick. And she didn't look scared…at all.

Bloody hell she's magnificent.

Amen.

Another bout of sick laughter emanated from Gavin. He had unquestionably lost it.

"Esme is alive, barely. I am here for the mongrel."

"Go to hell, Gavin," he shouted.

Enough of this. Shift now and we can help her fight.

"Oh, I have no problem with that. I feel I'll fit right in."

The wind started to howl again. The darkness seemed to grow around them, blotting out all the light. As they both watched in horror, dark figures appeared behind Gavin.

"You had to find creatures worse than you to fight."

"I only wanted what is mine."

Brody shook his head. He took Anice's hand and pressed the jewel into her palm. "Protect it."

She looked at the jewel, then back up at him.

"I love you, Anice McLennan. You are my heart, my soul, the only mate I could ever want."

He bent his head and pressed a quick, hard kiss to her lips before pulling back.

"Brody," Anice said.

He shook his head. "No time. Then, he stripped out of his clothes before he started to shift. His wolf was raring to go, to stand side by side with their mate and fight the evil.

Once he had completely transformed, he lunged at Gavin. He clawed at the bastard and felt satisfaction when he dug his claws into his flesh. The scream that rent the air was otherworldly and evil. It vibrated through the air as he pushed away from Brody. Brody hit the ground hard. Jarred by the impact, it took him a moment or two to gather his wits about him. By the time he did, Gavin was slithering toward Anice. Energy sparked as Gavin sent blasts in Anice's direction while he chased her.

"The jewel is mine. You must suffer."

He sounded mad. Ominous chanting started. It didn't come from Gavin. It filled the air around them as Anice came to an abrupt stop. Her panic hit him like a whip, lashing at his composure. He knew something had stopped her.

She turned to face Gavin, and he wanted to shout at

her to hide, to get down. Instead, she settled her hands on her hips and stared the bastard down.

His heart almost stopped beating.

Fear pushed him to move faster, even as the dark forces helping Gavin pressed against him, making it harder to move forward.

"The jewel is not yours," Anice screamed. "You have no right to anything. You and your entire line are thieving bastards who never accomplished anything."

She glanced in Brody's direction for a split second, and he knew that she was trapped but was giving Brody time to get to them.

Since Gavin had turned his back to Brody, and all of his attention was focused on Anice, Brody had an advantage. He rushed Gavin from behind, ignoring the nips of heat that flayed at his fur. He knew that Gavin had help, but Brody didn't let it stop him. He jumped on Gavin's back and sunk his fangs into Gavin's flesh. Gavin screamed and tried to get him off, but Brody used his claws to hang on tight.

"Get off me," he screamed, thrashing about enough to toss Brody off of him. Brody landed on his back, harder than his last fall. It knocked the air out of him for a few seconds.

"Mine!" Gavin's screech filled the night air.

Brody felt a shift in the atmosphere as he shook his head to clear it and rose to his paws. Now, the air around them seemed more turbulent, as if warring weather systems were in the skies above them.

Esme was rushing Gavin, who was completely focused on Anice now. This time, Brody approached him, then started to run to get another leap on him. Esme hit Gavin with some kind of magick that caused the bastard to stumble back and turn just as Brody took the leap off the ground. He slashed the other man across the face and chest before he disappeared into thin air. Brody fell to the ground and rolled over, jumping to his feet to face Gavin should he reappear. He didn't.

"Brody!" Anice called to him. He looked over to find her holding Esme as both women sunk down to the ground. He rushed forward.

"I'm okay. That just took a little out of me," Esme said, but her voice was weak.

"I think we should get her out of here," Anice said.

"You have the jewel?"

Anice nodded and reached into her pocket. "Gone."

At that moment, her phone buzzed. As she pulled it out, Brody shifted back to his human form. He knew he would have to probably carry Esme. He slipped on his jeans and had his shirt on when he looked over at Anice. Tears filled her eyes.

"What's wrong, love."

"It made it back," she said, laughing. "The amethyst appeared in the sword. It's over."

"That's good," Esme said before passing out. He hurried over and felt for her pulse. It was still there and strong.

"Let me find my shoes and I'll take her off your hands."

"Brody?" Anice asked.

"Yes?"

"Did you mean it?"

He looked at her and knew what she was asking. "I did."

She gave him a small smile, then looked back down at

Esme. "She's going to be very upset Gavin still has his bits and pieces on him."

He smiled. "She will."

"I guess we need to get Esme back."

He gave Anice a quick hard kiss, then slipped his arms beneath Esme and lifted her off the ground. They had a lot to talk about, things to work out, but getting Esme back so she could rest was important.

Gavin was wounded and dangerous to anyone who ventured into his path. Brody was sure he planned to confront Callum. Brody hoped Callum, and the rest of the McLennans and Stewarts, took care of Gavin once and for all.

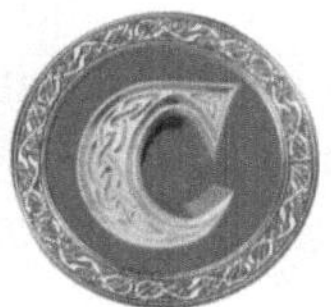

Chapter Eighteen

Callum and Phoebe were sitting in the dining room with everyone but the two remaining Stewarts, the sword was on the table when the flash happened. Magick charged the air, then the amethyst appeared. The sword vibrated.

"It's done," Callum said, grabbing the Claymore by the hilt. The power of the sword surged through him, along with the knowledge that they were finally free. "About bloody time."

"I texted Anice. They're all right."

"Good."

Before Phoebe could stand, there was a commotion outside. The front door blasted open, splintering inward. A rush of darkness seemed to seep into the house.

"Stay here," he said to Phoebe as he stepped out in the hallway with the sword in hand.

"Meg and Maggie, you stay here," he said. Meg opened her mouth to argue, but he said, "I need you here to protect Phoebe."

The weight of what he was asking her to do showed in

her gaze when she nodded. "I'll not let the bastard near her."

"Nor will I," Maggie said, as she turned to Belvidore and Jack. "Make sure you two stay down. This might get a little messy.

"Callum McLennan, come and face your doom."

"What the bloody hell does that mean?" Logan asked. "Who talks like that?"

"He's definitely lost it," Angus commented. Both of them were armed with swords themselves. Rena had told them not to use guns as bullets were easier to turn back against them.

Fletcher stepped up beside Callum. "Let's get this bastard."

Callum glanced back at his wife once more. Centuries he had been waiting for her and he wasn't giving her or their baby up.

"Doona get killed out there, you idiot," she said, her voice wavering just a bit, telling him how scared she was.

"I wouldna think of it, my love."

Then he turned and stepped out into the hallway. Gavin stood before him. His hair was a mess and his clothes seemed to have been torn to shreds. Brody had been after him. Callum wanted to know what happened to his cousin and all of their friends, but right now, he had to concentrate on the wreck of a man in front of him. He was there to kill Phoebe and their baby and him. He might not feel different, but he knew he was probably mortal at the moment.

"So, you have all the jewels," Gavin said, limping toward him. The doors to the dining room shut, and he knew his two cousins stood in front of it, both armed.

The sound of claws against the wooden floor came

from behind him. He knew without looking they were the Stewart brothers. He knew his cousins stood ready to lend a hand if needed. Anger and fear drove him—and them. He wasn't the only one who had a loved one in peril.

"He's mine," Callum said in warning. "But I doona mind the back up." There was a growl, and he was sure it was Cayden.

"Going to have your mongrels attack me?" Gavin asked as he limped forward.

"No. That's your way. None of you ever do the dirty work yourselves. This is all about you and me. McLennan against McWalton."

The smile that curved Gavin's lips made him appear even more evil, but Callum didn't care. In fact, it made him feel stronger. The witches were protecting his wife and baby, and Rena was there to lend a magickal helping hand if he needed.

He took the sword in one hand and then motioned with his other. A few seconds ticked by as the atmosphere grew heavier and the lights started to flicker. Callum was worried that Gavin wasn't going to fight him directly. He knew the witches and Serena would back him up, and Archie had said he would shift back into human form if need be. Still, Callum wanted this fight. He wanted to go one on one with Gavin. He was the representative of every bastard who'd made their lives hell for centuries.

"Come now, Gavin. Are you that much of a coward?" he asked, as he let his disdain for the present laird drip from every syllable.

There was a shimmer of magick in the air, but it was accompanied by the smell of Sulphur. He was surprised when Gavin screamed and ran straight at him. This was not the businessman he knew, the one who had been composed and cordial. This was a shell, controlled by the darkest of magick known to man.

Callum knew Gavin wasn't thinking straight or he would have protected himself better. Callum stepped out of the way, turning the sword so that he could slice his arm. The scream that filled the hallway sounded like a wounded animal.

It wasn't blood that dripped from his arm, but black goo, as if even his blood was tainted with the magick he'd been playing with. There was a growl behind Gavin from one of the wolves, and he noticed the creeping shadows coming down the hallway. Gavin hadn't come alone.

Wind started to blow through the house, rattling the various paintings on the walls. It was hot and oppressive, as if sucking all the rest of the air out of the house.

"I've got this," Rena said, and she started to move down the hallway, her hands outstretched and sparks of light coming off her fingertips.

"So, you do need your family."

"I know I need them. You didna come alone. At least I didna have to sell my soul to get support."

Another spark of heat zapped through the hallway. The force of it slammed Callum against the wall, his head smacking hard against it, but he held onto the sword—barely. Callum slid down to the floor as stars appeared before his eyes. The hit had left his body in pain—more than just a simple smack against the wall. The malicious taint to the magick left him aching, as if he had been through a battle Everyone seemed to be shouting at once, and the Stewarts were growling, but Callum took his time. He had to shake his head to clear it so that he was no longer seeing double.

He took a step and felt another brush of evil energy,

but this time it wasn't as strong. He glanced at Rena, who was still working hard against the magick, and she seemed to be gaining ground. The air was cleaner, if still tainted.

"So, you are a little man, Gavin. You have to have someone fight your battles."

"I say you have some help too," Gavin said, making a movement with his hand, and sending his cousins flying. They all hit the wall with a thud.

"We're okay," Angus said, getting nods from the other two.

"They are just there if you win. But you can't win if you doona have the bollocks to fight me. You have always been a coward, just like your predecessors."

"Fuck you."

Callum smiled. "Come and try it."

Gavin gave out another retched scream as he rushed toward Callum. At that moment, the air cleared up completely, the malevolent power shrinking away. His eyes bulged, and he had the look of someone who had gone completely mad. It had to be the reason he didn't notice Callum was ready for him. He held the sword steady as he met the bastard. The sword hit him true in the chest, piercing his heart. Gavin's eyes widened as he looked up at Callum. Callum pulled the sword back and watched the other man stagger back as he raised his hand to his chest. Just like before, instead of blood, blackness oozed out of his chest and over his hands. He fell against the floor, his head hitting the wood with a thud.

Both of the Stewart brothers bared their teeth and growled as they stood over the fallen laird. He assumed they were making sure the bastard stayed on the ground. Callum approached him, satisfaction laced with just a hint of regret. Not for the man lying on the floor dying. It was for the man he had been, before darkness had crept into his body and taken over.

"You know…I was supposed to win because I am stronger."

"You might be stronger on your own, but I have a family at my back, one who would stand by me. I didna need them to fight, but I knew they were there if I needed them. That is what McLennans stand for. Your lot will never understand that. Because of that, you'll die alone."

"Go to hell," he said, then his breathing grew raspy, the death rattle Callum had heard before. The door to the dining room burst open and the others rushed out. As they did, Gavin dissolved into the same black goo that had pumped out of his heart as he died. Abruptly, it seemed to dry up and disappear. There was only a faint scent of Sulphur in the air.

"It's safe," Logan yelled out, as the witches and Phoebe joined them.

"That's…bloody hell! It's over," Angus said as he picked up his wife and kissed her. Then he picked his son up and twirled him around. "It's all over, Jack."

The heaviness that had been holding them down since Gavin arrived completely dissolved. Clean air swept through the house again, and the lights brightened.

Callum wrapped his arms around Phoebe. "It's all because of you, love."

She pulled back and looked up at him. Tears streamed down her face and her nose was red. Panicked, he brushed them away.

"Doona cry, love."

She shook her head, smiling. "For happiness. I'm so relieved we are all okay."

He kissed her nose. "Like I said, all because of you, love."

"Callum," she said, apparently unable to continue as a fresh wave of tears poured down her cheeks. Knowing that if he said anymore, she might just get worse, he pulled her into his arms again and held on tight.

"We need to celebrate," Rena called out.

The Stewart brothers rejoined them in human form, thankfully dressed.

"It'll be at least three hours before Brody, Anice and Esme make it back," Cayden said.

"I'll take care of that," Rena said, and she disappeared.

"I'll never get used to that," Phoebe said with a laugh. "But I doona care."

Jack was giggling as he was tossed from cousin to cousin.

"Be careful with him," Maggie called out, but she was laughing too.

Callum laughed and kissed Phoebe. "Let's hunt something up to eat, and we are definitely opening some whisky tonight."

"Indeed, my lord," Belvidore said. "I made sure Cook made up some platters for tonight."

"What if I had been killed?" Callum asked.

"We would need it for the mourners," Belvidore said without cracking a smile.

Phoebe chuckled. "You can't say that he isn't prepared."

"No, and I am too bloody happy right now to care. To the kitchen everyone and make sure we have a few bottles of that whisky."

Chapter Nineteen

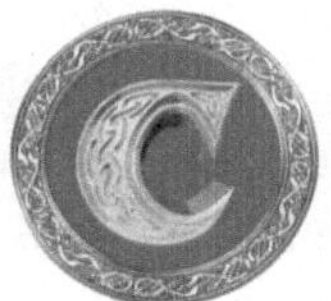

Time seemed to stand still as they tried to get home as fast as possible. Anice sat in the back seat with Esme's head in her lap. Her pulse and breathing were steady, but there was definitely something off with her. She was worried, and she knew that Brody was concerned. That made her worry even more.

They were about halfway home when Rena appeared in the passenger seat of the SUV.

"What's taking so bloody long?" she demanded, then she saw Esme. "I thought she was okay."

"She is. I think the fight just wiped her out."

Rena nodded, though her expression was no longer as light as it had been.

"I know I will regret this, but, pull over to the side of the road."

Brody found a spot and did as she ordered. Anice's worry increased tenfold. He was definitely worried since he was barely saying anything. He knew Esme better than either her or Rena, so he would probably know what was normal and what wasn't.

Rena waited for a car to speed by, then she closed her eyes. They reappeared in front of the mansion. It seemed like lights were on in every room. Rena must have sent some sort of signal that they were to arrive because the door was open, light pouring out of it. The entire family, along with their guests, came pouring out of the house. Brody was out of the car and opening Anice's door almost immediately. Cayden appeared behind him.

"How is she?" the Alpha asked.

"She's been out since the fight. Her pulse has been strong the whole time," Brody said, his gaze fixated on his cousin. "I'm going to lift her head, then you—"

Esme disappeared.

"Dammit."

"Waste of time and energy," Rena said. "She's in her room. Do you have a healer in your pack?"

"Esme is usually the healer, but she trained Archie."

"Let's go. I need to grab some things, and I know that the M and M's have started to get things prepared in her room now."

Rena turned and then wobbled a little. Fletcher caught her. "Careful, love. You expended a lot of energy."

She nodded and let him help her up the stairs to the front door. Anice stepped out of the SUV and found herself a little unsteady. Brody took her arm, then lifted her into his arms. Normally, she would have insisted that she walk, but she had no energy. The journey, the entire fight, had been a little too much. They arrived in the kitchen and Belvidore had a cup of tea ready for her and Brody.

"I put a little whisky in it for you both," he said, giving Brody the seal of approval.

They sipped on their tea and ate some biscuits as they

told the story, then listened to what happened here at the house.

"He just disappeared?" she asked.

Callum nodded. "Actually, it was more like he dissolved into the black junk he was made up of."

She sighed. "It's over. I doona feel any different though."

"Maybe tomorrow," Brody said, slipping his arm around her and pulling her closer. They sat together on the bench. She should probably object, but it felt too good having his arms wrapped around her in such a manner. His body warmth comforted her, and she could swear she heard his heart beating.

Maggie appeared at the door, a smile on her face. "Esme is doing fine, and she would like to see her stupid boy cousins—her name for them, not mine. She's a little tired, but she'll just need a little rest. With two resident witches and Archie around, along with Rena, we'll have her back up on her feet in no time."

Cayden stood and headed toward the door, but she sensed Brody's hesitation. He didn't want to leave her.

"Go. I'll still be here when you return."

"Okay," he said, leaning down to brush his mouth over hers. "We need to talk."

She nodded, knowing he was right. Since Fletcher, Logan, and Angus, along with Jack, had gone upstairs, she was now alone with Callum and Phoebe. Phoebe scooted closer, then motioned with her head to Callum.

"I'll be back in a bit," he said, kissing his wife, then kissing the top of Anice's head. "Glad you made it back to us, love." Then he left them alone.

"So, everything is over."

"I wouldn't say that," Phoebe said. "Tomorrow, all of

you could wake up and look like you were almost three hundred years old."

"Phoebe!"

"I'm sorry, but that has always been a worry of mine. Thankfully, I translated a passage in the last hour that told me differently."

"The last hour? Good lord."

"Yes. I just needed to read the diary. I wasn't sure why, but it was right there when I needed to read it. "

"What did it say?"

She pulled out a piece of paper. "You're the first person I'm telling about this."

"Thank you."

"Seeing that you are the entire reason this all happened, I thought you should get this first. Once the stones are returned, the five will be free of the curse that has entrapped them. With their past behind them, they can take comfort in the knowledge that they will lead peaceful lives as mortals. They have earned that, and more."

For a long moment she blinked. "That's it? No...we will slap you again if you should do something we doona like?"

Phoebe chuckled. "No. Nothing that exciting. Although, there is a ton of the book I still need to work on."

"Those bloody barmy witches. Now that we put you through the damned wringer, see you later," Anice said laughing, but it soon ended on a sob.

"Oh, love," Phoebe said, pulling her into her arms.

She was embarrassed, but she couldn't stop herself from crying. All the years of not knowing, of thinking they would never have normal lives. Now that it was over, she really didn't know why she felt so overwhelmed.

"Anice, sweetheart, it's going to be okay."

She pulled back and took the tissue Phoebe offered her.

"I know, I just…" another sob caught her unawares.

"What the bloody hell is going on in here?" Brody demanded. She turned to face him, and another sob hit her. "What did you do to her?"

"Nothing at all," Phoebe said, humor lacing her voice.

"Well, she's crying, so you had to do something."

"She didn't do anything," Anice said, wiping her tears away.

Callum came in, a frown marring his face. Well, that was normal, but apparently, it wasn't as normal as it had been at one time because Anice noticed it.

"There you are, love. I'm ready to go up to bed."

Callum blinked. "Of course," he said, helping her up and then out of the kitchen. He tossed a dirty look over his shoulder to Brody. Anice guessed it was some kind of warning.

Brody slipped into the empty space next to her. "So, love, want to tell me what this is all about?"

She shrugged. "Not really sure. Phoebe and I were talking and just…it's a lot."

He nodded.

"How's Esme?"

"Awake, better. She's still really weak."

Then silence. Neither of them seemed to know what to say next.

"Brody."

"Yes?"

Anice's thoughts were a jumbled mess. How could she tell him how she felt about him? What they had been through was so overwhelming that it seemed so silly to worry about things like this. So she decided to just keep it simple.

"I…I never answered you when you said you loved me."

"It didn't need an answer. I wanted you to know that I loved you just in case something happened to me. It didn't require a response."

She studied him for a long moment. The truth was right there in his eyes. The same eyes she had seen when he had shifted. Both Brody the man and Brody the shifter loved her. He would fight by her side against any foe, and she had no doubt he would lay down his life for her.

"What happens to mates who are not wolves?"

He cocked his head to the side studying her. "Why?"

"Humor me."

He shrugged. "Nothing really. Some do choose to be bloodied."

"That means turned into a wolf?"

He nodded. "But not everyone can."

"What about the offspring?"

"Esme is a prime example of that. Her mother was full witch and her father was half witch and half wolf like my family. Sometimes, though, they will be able to shift."

She cupped his face. "I love you, Brody Stewart. You're an ass for lying to me, but I understand how important family is."

"When?" he asked.

"When what?"

"When did you realize you loved me?"

"A while ago, but the one thing I realized when we were fighting Gavin was that, other than my family, you were the person I wanted by my side. I wanted you to be with me every step of the way."

For a long moment he said nothing, then, his mouth curved into a delicious smile. "I doona want it any other way, love. Marry me. Be my mate."

She smiled dropping her hands and leaning closer. "I will, Brody. Now and forever, I'm yours."

Anice kissed him, her heart full of joy knowing that they were finally all free.

Epilogue

Six months later...

Callum looked over the ballroom from the doorway, as the new bride and groom danced. It was the first big family celebration at their new home on McLennan land. Things had definitely changed since the curse had been broken, all of them for the better.

None of the cousins really had issues. Anice had made jokes that all of them would probably develop arthritis over night, but nothing that dire had happened. Of course, Fletcher getting his first real gray hair had been fun for all of them.

He shook his head. Everything was going well for all of them, including Anice. She smiled up at Brody, tears in her eyes as they danced around the ballroom. Callum had had the honor of walking her down the aisle just a few hours earlier. She had been more nervous than Callum, not once faltering in her vows, and she'd had a smile the entire ceremony.

The rest of the Stewarts had returned to Scotland,

their family having inherited the old family land. Cayden had taken control of it, making sure to get the rest of the pack back to Scotland, all except for their sister. She had returned for the wedding, but Callum knew the leggy brunette would be on her way back to Texas next week. Esme was recovered from her injuries, but she seemed somehow different than before. They each were to some extent, but the witch still had the sharp wit they all loved. She had become a regular fixture in their house, hanging out with the M and M's, conjuring all sorts of mischief.

"You're skulking about," Phoebe said, stepping up beside him. He looked down at her and their son. Ian was only five months old, but he had become the most important person in both their lives.

"I'm not. I'm observing happiness."

She smiled. "We have that in spades these days."

"Definitely."

"Did you talk to Logan?" she asked.

"Yes. I have a feeling you knew that Meghan was expecting already?"

"It's the kind of thing women like to tell each other." She sighed. He motioned with his hands and she gave him Ian. He held his son in one hand and wrapped his arm around Phoebe, pulling her against his side.

Not for the first time since they had broken the curse, Callum let happiness fill his soul. His family... his love... all the things that were important were there, and he would always know the importance of both. He looked down at Phoebe, who brushed a tear away.

"Doona be sad, love."

She smiled up at him. "I'm not. I'm just happy and I love you."

"I love you too," he said, leaning down to kiss her. The

room apparently noticed and broke out in applause and laughter. He raised up and looked over the crowd again, then back to his wife. "Shall we?"

He didn't have to explain. She smiled and nodded. With his arm still wrapped around her, they walked into the room, their lives at peace and their family complete.

A Note from Mel

Thank you so much for reading Anice and Brody's story. I truly appreciate that you took the time and I hope that you enjoyed it. If you did, please think of leaving a review and telling your friends about the book.

I know that many of you might want to know about the Stewarts and if they will get their own series. If you would truly like to see the series published, be sure to let me know on Facebook, Twitter, or email me. Tell me if you would like to read all about the family of shifters.

I do have a few more paranormal books, but one series I love, love, love, is my **BY BLOOD.** Step into Victorian England where an entire class of vampires operate within the glittering ton. Make sure to check out the **WORLD GUIDE** on my website!

About the Author

From an early age, USA Today Best-selling author Melissa loved to read. First, it was the books her mother read to her including her two favorites, Winnie the Pooh and the Beatrix Potter books. She cut her preteen teeth on Trixie Belden and read and reviewed To Kill a Mockingbird in middle school. It wasn't until she was in college that she tried to write her first stories, which were full of angst and pain, and really not that fun to read or write. After trying several different genres, she found romance in a Linda Howard book.

Since her first published book, Grace Under Pressure, Mel has had over 60 short stories, novellas, and novels published. She has written in genres ranging from historical to contemporary to futuristic and has worked with 8 publishers although she handles most of her publishing herself. She is best known for her Harmless and Santini series.

After years of following her military husband around the country and world, Mel happily lives with her family in horse and wine country in Northern Virginia.

Keep up with Mel, her releases, and her appearances

by subscribing to her <u>NEWSLETTER</u> or join in the fun with her Harmless Addicts!

Mel's Facebook Series Pages
The Cursed Clan
Task Force Hawaii
The Harmless Series
The Santinis
Semper Fi Marines

Check out Mel's Storyboards on Pinterest

For more info:
www.melissaschroeder
melissa@melissaschroeder.net

facebook.com/MelissaSchroederfanpage

twitter.com/melschroeder

instagram.com/melschro

bookbub.com/authors/melissa-schroeder

pinterest.com/melissaschro

Callum

Angus

Logan

Fletcher

Anice

BY BLOOD

Desire by Blood

Seduction by Blood

BOUNTY HUNTER'S, INC

For Love or Honor

Sinner's Delight

TELEPATHIC CRAVINGS

Voices Carry

Lost in Emotion

Hard Habit to Break

Bundle

CONNECTED BOOKS

The Hired Hand

Hands on Training

A Calculated Seduction

Going for Eight

9 781939 734808